Feisty
PRINCESS

A SEXY MANHATTAN FAIRYTALE: PART TWO

Michelle A. Valentine

Leighann —

Princesses Rule —

♡

Michelle A Valentine

Contents

Books by
Michelle A. Valentine

The Black Falcon Series
ROCK THE BEGINNING
ROCK THE HEART
ROCK THE BAND
ROCK MY BED
ROCK MY WORLD
ROCK THE BEAT
ROCK MY BODY
Hard Knocks Series
PHENOMENAL X
XAVIER COLD (Releases: January 20th)
The Collectors Series
DEMON AT MY DOOR
COMING SOON—DEMON IN MY BED
A Sexy Manhattan Fairytale
NAUGHTY KING
FIESTY PRINCESS
COMING SOON—DIRTY ROYALS
• **Wicked White Series**
WICKED WHITE
WICKED REUNION (Releases December
15th)

Chapter I
DUM-DA-DA-DUN

Margo

I STARE AT THE WEDDING photo in absolute horror. "Oh, my God. Yamada was a witness? And is he wearing—" I lean in and take a closer look "—an Elvis costume?"

Alexander leans over my shoulder while I sit at the island in the kitchen of our suite, his spicy scent wafting around me as he gets a better view. "Shit." He pushes himself back upright and straightens the dark blue tie he's wearing. Even in a dress shirt, the man makes my mouth water.

I gaze up to see a pair of gray eyes trained on me. "Please tell me this is all a sick joke. Please tell me that we aren't really married."

"No joke, Dime Piece," Yamada says as he walks into the common area of the suite with a set of brunette twins wearing matching schoolgirl outfits—one under each arm. "Yamada was there, and it was the dopest wedding ever! Wasn't it, ladies?"

The two women giggle and nod in agreement. One even runs her finger suggestively over Yamada's scrawny bare chest beneath the silk robe he's still wearing. "Whatever you say, baby," the woman purrs.

Yamada grabs the woman's hand. "No touching in front of Dime Piece. Might make her jealous. Poor girl will never get a taste of a night with Yamada since she's married to King now."

The woman jerks her gaze to me, and I swear to God she hisses at me. I raise my eyebrows, and Alexander shakes his head.

"We need to talk about what happened last night, Yamada," Alexander tells him and then adds, "*Alone.*"

"Okay," Yamada says and then gives each of his companions a kiss on the cheek. "Time to go, lovelies."

"But we want to play with Yamada some more," one of the girls whines in a voice that mimics a toddler as Yamada turns them both toward the door.

He opens the door and ushers the girls out, patting each one on the butt as they pass him. "Sorry, but Yamada's a man in demand. Bye girls."

"Yamada . . ." the girls' voice cuts off as he shuts the door in their faces.

He turns and gives us a mischievous grin. "Bitches love Yamada."

Alexander rolls his eyes. "I have no idea why."

"Don't be a hater." Yamada struts into the kitchen and opens the door on the stocked refrigerator, reaching in for a bottle of juice. He twists the cap off his apple juice and then halts when he turns to take in the expression on Alexander's face. "Why are you not the happiest madafaka on the planet right now? You're married to the hottest chick Yamada has ever seen. What's there not to be happy about?"

Alexander folds his arms over his chest. "This isn't funny. What the hell happened last night?"

Yamada swallows and then shrugs. "We were all having fun. The two of you were fucked-up and when we passed a wedding chapel . . ."

"And let me guess. You convinced us in our drunken state that it would be so much fun," Alexander finishes for him.

Yamada's face pulls into a lopsided grin. "You didn't take much convincing."

Before Alexander has a chance to respond, the front door pops open and the same bodyguard with the braids who walked me up to Yamada's party last night sticks his head through the door. "Sorry to disturb you, Mr. Yamada, but we have a situation. The women you escorted out are sitting in front of the elevator demanding to speak with you about when they can see you again. Would you like us to physically remove them from the property, sir?"

"Let me talk to them." Yamada shakes his head, muttering as he heads toward the door. "This happens every time."

"Yamada . . ."Alexander calls after his friend but gets no response as the door closes us alone in the suite.

Alexander turns around and rests his back against the counter in the kitchen area of our suite. The material of his pressed shirt strains against his bicep as he lifts his hand to pinch the bridge of his nose while he squeezes his eyes shut. "I can't believe I allowed you to con me into this. How could I be so careless?"

This causes me to jerk my eyebrows up as my eyes widen. "Me? You actually think I *want* to be married to you?"

His eyes snap open. He holds up his left hand that's still bearing a wedding ring and points to it. "Obviously, you do. You don't honestly expect me to believe that Yamada came up with that shit by himself. He had to get the idea from somewhere."

"Excuse me." I lift my hand to interrupt. This man is completely out of his ever-lovin' mind if he believes that. "Being married to you is the last thing on my wish list. Why would I ever subject myself to something like that?"

Alexander releases a bitter laugh. "Right. I know you're smarter than that, Margo, so cut the act."

My mouth falls open. "What *act*? My thorough disgust at the thought of being your wife isn't for show—that I can assure you. My disdain for you is quite real."

He stares at me through narrowed eyes. "I'm sure you'd like me to believe that, but Princess, I'm on to your game. Once Jack figures out if we're legally married, I'll have him slap you with an annulment so fast it'll make your head spin. When I told you to marry some schmuck for money, I didn't mean me!"

The moment those words leave his mouth, things begin clicking into place. My hungover brain obviously isn't quick enough this morning to figure out that if, in fact, we are married, it means there was no time for any pesky contracts like a prenuptial agreement. Alexander King is screwed, and he knows it. He's now at my mercy.

Oh, how the tables have turned.

Since he paints me to be the evil mastermind of this plot, I might as well go along with it.

I lick my lips and peer into the beautiful eyes of the man I love to hate. "I must say, Alexander, this new development changes things drastically between us. Don't you think?"

"This changes nothing," he growls. "This marriage is a mistake. No judge in the world will award you shit if you press the issue. Besides, we don't even know if the marriage is legal." He snatches the picture of the so-called wedding off the table and panic rolls through his voice. "A minister wearing a fucking Kiss costume can't be a legitimate man of the cloth capable of marrying people legally, right?"

While I have to agree with him on that, there's no way I'm about to let Alexander know that I'm having a hard time believing this whole thing is legit.

"Maybe you're right . . ." I tilt my head. "And maybe you're wrong. Are you willing to take a chance and find out? If our marriage is legally binding, I won't let you off easy."

There's a long pause of silence between us, and I can tell the wheels are spinning inside that brain of his, He's trying to figure a way out of this situation.

"What will it take for you to walk away from this quietly?" Alexander's nostrils flare, and I can't help smiling. Pissing him off is my new favorite pastime.

I turn on the barstool that I'm occupying and cross my legs in the direction that Alexander is standing. It's finally nice to feel like the one in control of this situation. For a while there, I felt like trying to save Buchanan Industries was a lost cause, but now things have definitely changed in my favor.

"You know exactly what I want," I tell him.

He raises his eyebrow. "Forget it. I have too much riding on this Buchanan deal. I'll take my chances with Jack eating you alive in court."

"Suit yourself. Everything that went on here this weekend will prove that you were a willing participant. Besides, your college buddy was your best man. Yamada wouldn't let someone coerce you into something that you weren't willing to do. I'm sure it won't be too hard to convince a judge to see things my way." I shrug and then push myself off the barstool. "I think I'll go ahead and start with a call to our family attorney. I'll have to start planning how I want to spend my newfound fortune of half your money."

"I don't know what planet you're living on, Margo, but that isn't going to happen." His gray eyes harden. "You can't afford to take me on."

"What's yours is mine, darling. So it seems to me like I can, thanks to your sprawling wealth."

His nostrils flare. "You are such a bitch. I can't believe for one moment that I—" He quickly cuts himself off and clenches his hands into fists by his sides. "Pack your shit. We're going back to New York. Now."

I fold my arms over my chest. "You can't tell me what to do."

Alexander smirks. "Being your husband earns me that right. Now pack."

I open my mouth to tell him to take his orders and shove them right up his bossy ass, but before I have a chance, he turns and walks toward his room, slamming the door behind him.

The second I'm sure that I'm alone, I drop my head and rub my forehead to try to soothe the pounding headache that's still raging inside. How the hell could I allow myself to get this out of control last night? I have so much riding on saving the family business. Being married to Alexander might fuck everything up.

Chapter II
CHANGE OF PLANS

Alexander

THE ROAR OF THE JET has been the only sound I've heard for the last hour. Margo hasn't said a word to me since we left Las Vegas. Hell, she hasn't even so much as glanced at me either. Whatever little connection we shared this weekend is now long gone. Reality has definitely set in that we are enemies and nothing more.

I allowed myself to forget that this weekend. I gave in to temptation and had her over and over.

It had been a long time since I'd laughed—let loose and just had a good time. The combination of liquor and Yamada tends to put me in a carefree state, but I never let my guard down around women. Margo Buchanan is irresistible, and I'm not exactly in the habit of telling myself no, which is how I landed myself in this situation. I couldn't get enough of her.

"Another scotch, Mr. King?" Abigail asks, pulling me out of my thoughts.

"Yes, but make it a double this time," I instruct her before she scampers off to fulfill my order.

I lay my head back against the headrest and close my eyes, only to be instantly alerted to a ringing phone. I answer on the second ring. "King."

"Madafaka! You left without telling Yamada good-bye?"

I roll my eyes. I knew he'd be pissed at me for taking off like that, but I couldn't spend one more minute in the penthouse cooped up with Margo's tempting ass. That woman and her sexy as sin body drives me out of my mind and causes me to lose all control, so I knew I had to get out of there before I did something foolish. I will not break down and give in to her demands, no matter how hard my dick gets.

But Yamada doesn't need to know that was my reason for taking off so quickly. "I'm sorry, my friend. I had urgent business I had to attend to back in New York."

He chuckles on the other end of the line. "You left because being alone with Margo scares the shit out of you. You forget how well Yamada knows you."

The tie around my neck feels too tight, so I pull it away from my skin to relieve the sudden choking sensation. "I assure you, that isn't the case."

"Uh-huh. Then you have no problem flying out to see Yamada on his private island on Thursday."

"A private island? When did you buy a fucking island? That's not really your scene."

"Everywhere Yamada chooses to be is Yamada's scene. Besides, it was a good investment. Everyone loves the British Virgin Islands. This place has a resort on it and a full staff. There are some fly honies that work there. We'll have a good time. No visitors on the island while Yamada's there either."

I rub my temple as I groan. "Now isn't really a good time. I have to sort out this crazy Vegas wedding you got me wrapped up in."

"Now is the perfect time," he chimes in. "We never talked business in Vegas. If you want Yamada Enterprises in on the Buchanan deal, then we sit down before Yamada goes back to Japan. Oh, and bring Dime Piece too or no deal."

"Yamada . . ."

"No is not an answer Yamada will respond to. You want to talk business, you come Thursday to see my new island. Yamada's Booty Paradise has a nice ring to it, no?" A female giggle cuts over the line and Yamada chuckles and then shushes her. "Got to go, King. I'll text you the island coordinates. See you Thursday."

"No. Wait. Yamada—" Silence is all I'm met with, and I curse as I hang up the phone.

A few seconds later, he sends coordinates to one of the small pieces of land in the British Virgin Islands via text.

I scrub both hands down my face. I'm not blind as to what Yamada is trying to do. His matchmaking between Margo and me isn't going to work. I'm not interested in a relationship, and Margo hates my guts, so I know she doesn't want one with me either. Earlier today, she clearly showed her disdain about being married to me. I know she won't appreciate Yamada's meddling with our lives any more than I do.

I jerk my gaze over to Margo. She chose to take the seat across the aisle instead of bravely facing me as she did on the way out here. In her current seat, her head faces away from me, causing me to take note of her striking profile. Her dark hair is pulled back in a low-set ponytail and those dark-rimmed glasses that she tends to wear around the office covers her eyes. Even when she doesn't seem to be trying to attract my attention, she always manages to capture it. She's really one of the most beautiful creatures I've ever seen.

Too bad she's also one of the biggest bitches on the planet.

"Bad news." She whips her head in my direction and meets my gaze. "It seems that Yamada has requested my presence at a private island this week."

Margo clutches her chest in dramatic shock. "That sounds *so* horrible for you. A private island? You *poor* thing. How will you ever survive?"

The sarcasm isn't missed in her voice, and it only makes me want to burst her little attitude bubble. "Trust me. It will be a complete fucking nightmare, especially since he says that I have to bring you along."

I fully expect her to get pissed and start shouting about all the reasons that she can't possibly accompany me to this island, but she doesn't do that. Instead, a wicked smile crosses her face. Instantly, that irritates me off. I don't like that she's pleased about this one damn bit.

"I don't know why you're so happy about this," I grumble.

That only causes her smile to widen. "Just means that Yamada is starting to like me too. I told you that he would be my friend."

My nostrils flare at that thought, but I know that no matter what Margo Buchanan believes, Yamada would never take her side over mine.

"When do we leave?" she asks.

"Yamada apparently owns one of the islands next to the British Virgin Islands, so it'll take us about six hours to fly there. Then we'll need to get a helicopter or boat to take us over to wherever this place is. If I want to make a deal with Yamada, then we have no other choice but to go. Once Yamada gets his mind stuck on something, he tends to get his way."

"Looks like the game is still on when it comes to Yamada," Margo muses.

It's time to remind her that I'm still the boss in this situation. "Don't get your hopes up, Princess. Yamada will never sign a deal with you over me. He's *my* friend."

She lifts her eyebrow. "You're not the only one who got an invite to chat, King, so it looks like he's my friend, too."

Dammit. I hate that she's right. Yamada does like her or else he would have never been so welcoming once he figured out that he wasn't getting into her pants. That also means this could be big trouble for me if she can figure out a way to sweet talk him in to doing a deal directly with her father instead of me. It will cost me far too much money and I won't allow that to happen.

When we land at the airstrip just outside the city, Margo rushes off the plane. She demanded that I order a car to be waiting for her because she refused to be trapped with me any longer than she had to. She doesn't even glance in my direction as she heads toward it.

Guess the fucking honeymoon's over.

I shove myself up from the smooth leather seat and button my jacket as I make my way off the plane. The late afternoon sun hits me full force as I step outside, causing me to whip out a pair of sunglasses from my inside pocket and then slide them on my face.

It's then that I notice Jack leaning against the limo with his arms crossed as he waits for me. Even though his sunglasses shield his eyes, the smirk on his face tells me that I've opened myself up to a never-ending line of jokes about my random Vegas nuptials. "Your wife isn't riding with us?"

I shake my head. "Don't start your shit."

"What?" Jack says with a slight chuckle as I slide into the limo first with him following right behind me. "I'm not allowed to ask about your wife?"

"She's not my wife," I snap.

This only causes Jack to laugh harder. "Sure, she is. It's legal and everything."

"Fuck." It's the only word that comes to mind. I'm totally fucked here. "How bad is it?"

Jack raises his eyebrows. "Well, if the two of you didn't consummate your marriage, I'm sure we could've had a quick annulment, but—" I pull my glasses off and give him my best you know me better than that look which cuts him off. "That's what I thought. We fight it. I'm not exactly a divorce lawyer, but I'm sure we can bring on a few other attorneys who specialize in high-profile cases to help. We might stand a chance."

"A chance?" There's a catch in my voice. "You have got to be fucking kidding me! You're telling me that after being married for one fucking day, it possible Margo Buchanan can take me to the fucking cleaners? This is fucking insane."

"Buddy, what's insane is you marrying a woman who's out for your blood. What possessed you to do it? I mean, I know she's hot, but was fucking her really worth all this trouble? What the hell were you thinking?"

I pinch the bridge of my nose. "I don't know."

I wish I could blame marrying Margo solely on Yamada, but I know that wouldn't be exactly fair. Being with Margo this weekend was exciting. She didn't take my shit, and I find that insanely attracted. Hell, maybe Jack can plead a case of temporary insanity because the woman causes me to lose my damn mind. Yamada said it didn't take much convincing for me to marry Margo, and in my gut, I know that's probably true. I drank enough liquor to kill a horse, so I know the logical part of my brain was not functioing, and my dick did any major decision-making.

I lift my head and stare out the window as the car cuts through traffic, getting us closer to Manhattan. "How quickly can we get this resolved?"

"Well, that depends," Jack replies.

"On . . ." I prod as I whip my gaze in his direction.

He sighs. "On whether or not Margo Buchanan cooperates."

I release a bitter laugh. "She hates me, so that won't happen."

"That's too bad. Dragging things out can cause problems. If the board catches wind about your fly-by-night nuptials, they may begin to question your integrity."

"My *integrity*? Are you fucking serious? This little mishap with Margo has nothing to do with my ability to run King Corporation. This business means more to me than anything else." I shake my head, reeling from the disbelief that Jack's even bringing this up. "I would rather slice off my own hand than do something to damage the empire my father built."

"I know that, but the board . . . they don't know you like I do, and well, you've amassed quite a reputation in this city when it comes to women. The board may perceive your rash decision to marry Margo and then immediately divorce her as you being a bit . . . flighty."

I raise one eyebrow. "Me . . . *flighty*? I'm an emanate professional. Why does who I fuck and accidentally marry bring my character into question?"

Jack shrugs. "It could cause them to question your decision-making skills—your ability to see what's best for the company in the long haul—and they may band together to try to go against you on things."

"That won't matter. I own a majority of this company. If they don't like the direction I take this business—tough. It's *my* fucking company."

"It is," Jack agrees. "I'm not bringing this up to be a prick, but I just want you to be aware. The board can make things a whole lot more difficult if they fight you on every little thing."

I run my fingers down the back of my neck and take a deep breath. Fuck. If only I could rewind time and go back to the first moment I fucked Margo and let my guard down, then none of this would be an issue right now. I screwed up, and now I have to deal with the consequences of giving in to my dark desires and taking Margo, even though I knew it could fuck everything up.

I meet Jack's stare. "So what should I do? If Margo refuses a quick annulment, there's no way I can keep this quiet and keep the word from spreading across this city. You know how people talk around here."

"Play nice with her," Jack says as if it's the simplest thing in the world. "Find out what it will take to appease her and give it to her so she doesn't fight you on this divorce."

"I can't do that!" I protest. "She wants me to bail out Buchanan Industries so her family's company won't go under, but you and I both know that if we do that, we'd lose millions on that deal. We can't afford to do that."

"Then you'll have to find a way to meet in the middle. You both are going to have to give a little to find common ground in this situation."

I scrub my hand down my face. This is horse shit. I hate the fact that she basically has my balls in her purse, ready to zip them in tight and cause me excruciating pain. I so badly want to bash my fucking head against the window as straight-up punishment for allowing shit to get out of control like this.

This—the whole allowing someone to gain the upper hand on me, especially a female—is not like me. I'm typically in control.

My cell rings and I fish it out of my jacket pocket before checking the caller ID. I sigh as I hit the green button, ready for the whine fest that I know my baby sister is about to inflict on me for missing her birthday party this weekend. "Yes, Diem?"

"Are you back in town yet?" she quizzes.

"Just landed about ten minutes ago," I tell her. I decide then that I might as well open the door for her temper tantrum for being absent this weekend. "How was your birthday party?"

"It was wonderful," she replies in a tone I only remember her using after watching some sappy romance movie. Most people would call it dreamy. I call it delusional. Diem is very much the hopeless romantic type, so this mood of hers tells me that she's met a guy.

I pinch the bridge of my nose. What shitty timing for this to happen. With me being so wrapped up in the whole Margo scandal and trying to close this deal with Yamada, I won't have time to properly investigate whoever this man is like I typically do. As her brother, I find that it's my duty to make sure whatever asshole is sniffing around my sister is good enough. Unfortunately, Diem tends to pick the loser artist types who I fear are after far more than her model good looks. Like me, people try to get their hooks in Diem for what our father left us, and it's up to me to protect my free-spirited, trusting sister from motherfuckers who would use her.

Time to cut to the chase.

"Who's the guy?"

"Does a man have to be involved for me to be happy?" Diem instantly fires back.

"Come on, Diem. You can't bullshit me. You know the drill. Who's the guy?"

She's quiet for a few moments and then says, "I'm not telling you."

"Diem . . ." I say her name with a bite of warning in my voice. "You might as well do this the easy way and just tell me. Don't make me have Jack start looking into who this mystery guy is you obviously don't want me to know about."

Jack's eyes immediately cut over to me at the mention of his name. I see a flicker of unease on his face before he quickly turns his head to stare out the side window. Jack hates when I send him out on personal missions like this for me—that's no secret—so I'm sure the idea of tracking down my kid sister's new love interest isn't something that he really wants to do. But I know Jack. He's loyal, and he'll do it if I ask him to because, not only does he work for me, but he's also my best friend.

"Don't do that," Diem begs. "I promise I'll tell you all about him when I'm ready, but for now, allow me to keep this to myself. Please, Alexander."

Her bravery to maintain this secret takes me aback because Diem isn't typically like that with me. Sure, she bucks against my will most of the time, but it doesn't take me long to get her to bend. She knows that I get what I want no matter what. So this little show of defiance catches me off guard, but the idea that she's finally growing a little backbone makes me proud in an odd way. It doesn't make me worry any less, though.

I sigh. "Fine. I won't push for now. But so help me, Diem, if this asshole hurts you in any way, I will end him."

"Thank you." The pleased tone in her voice rings through loud and clear.

After I tell her good-bye, I end the call and lean my head back against the headrest. I hope Diem knows what she's doing and doesn't do anything rash with this guy until I've had time to run a full background check on him. I don't have time to worry about my sister right now though. I have to focus all my energy on figuring out how to get out of the fucking mess I've gotten myself into with Margo. I can't believe I'm married to the fucking Feisty Princess of Manhattan. How in the hell did I allow this to happen?

Chapter III
MOTHER KNOWS BEST

Margo

IT TAKES EVERYTHING IN ME not to bash my head against the expensive marble counter as I sit at the island in my mother's ridiculously huge kitchen. I'm trying to figure out a way to tell her that I married a total rat-bastard this weekend on accident. Seriously, when Jean Paul renovated his Upper East Side apartment, he spared no expense when it came to this kitchen. It makes sense because he does occasionally film segments of his television show in here.

"That man takes such good care of me." Mother busies herself with punching reheat on two of the pre-cooked meals her husband prepared for her in his absence. "He won't leave for a trip if he hasn't left food for me to heat up while he's gone." She turns to face me with a dreamy expression on her face. "I really think I've found a good one this time, Margo, honey. This one is a keeper."

I love my mother, but it takes everything in me not to roll my eyes and blurt out 'that's what you said about the last four.' My mother is a hopeful romantic, always believing in soul mates and fate and all that hokey nonsense.

She takes in the expression on my face and then shakes her head, causing her long dark curls to bounce around her shoulders. "Don't give me that look."

My mouth drops. Sometimes I forget how good she is at reading what's on my mind even if I don't make a move to voice it. "I didn't say anything."

"You didn't have to. I'm your mother, Margo. I can read how much you detest the idea of love by the expression on your face. I'm pretty good at that, you know. Matter-of-fact, I once had this clairvoyant tell me I was a natural at reading auras." The sound of the microwave dings, signaling that our food is ready and interrupting her train of thought. She lifts one of the plates of grilled chicken to her nose. "Ah. This smells wonderful. Jean Paul is a man of many talents, cooking being one of them." She wiggles her eyebrows suggestively.

My face twists. "Ew. Mother. Please. I'm your child, for God's sake. I don't need to hear about your sex life."

She sets a plate in front of me and then waves me off dismissively. "Oh, please, darling. You're a grown woman. It's not like you are too young to hear about this."

I wrinkle my nose as I cut into the chicken in front of me. "There's never going to be an age when I'm old enough to discuss sex with you."

Mother pulls out the barstool across from me and takes a seat before she begins to cut up her food. "Speaking of sex, I took the liberty of Googling Alexander King while you were off gallivanting with him last week."

I raise one eyebrow as I swallow down the food in my mouth and do my best not to choke. "Why would you do that?"

"I had to see exactly who my daughter was spending all her time with."

This time, I do roll my eyes. "Don't let his beautiful face fool you. He's not pleasant to be around."

"The hot ones never are, dear. That's what makes them so fun. They're a challenge." A smile pulls at the corners of her mouth. She's no doubt reliving some memory of a time she spent with some old asshole boyfriend as she takes a sip of her water. "Tell me, was that trip to Vegas all work or did you manage to get some playtime in with the notorious Naughty King?"

For a moment, I debate whether to lie to her. I could stick to the story that absolutely nothing happened between Alexander and me, but knowing how well she can read me, she'll see right through me.

I readjust in my seat. "I would like to say that it was all business . . ."

"But?" she prods.

"It wasn't," I answer honestly.

Her smile widens as she leans in, clamoring for the juicy bit of gossip she can tell is about to spill out of my mouth. "Do tell. And don't leave out one sordid detail."

I close my eyes and wrinkle my nose. There's no way I can hide what happened in Vegas from her. Besides, she's the one person in this world I can trust with this secret. "I slept with him."

"That's my girl!" she exclaims and then instantly launches into a question. "How was it?"

"Mother!"

"What? Inquiring minds, darling. Are you going to see him again?"

I lift one shoulder in a noncommittal shrug. "I don't want to, but I'm afraid I'll be forced to."

She nods. "That's right. The whole spy mission your father has you on. I nearly forgot about that. If you really don't want to see Alexander King anymore, just quit and tell your father that you're done being his little tattletale. Lord knows how hard it is to be in close proximity to an ex-lover. Your father should understand and not make too much of a fuss over the situation."

I sigh. "It's not that simple, I'm afraid."

"But it is. If you're afraid to tell your father, I'll call and tell—"

"My issues are much bigger than handling Daddy."

She bunches her brow, clearly confused. I can see the wheels turning behind her eyes as she tries to figure out what I'm hiding. "Then what is it?"

"I married the bastard on a drunken whim," I blurt out before I lose my nerve.

Her eyes widen. "Say again? I'm not sure I heard that quite right. It sounded like you just told me that my only child ran off to Vegas and got married for the very first time without me present."

My lips twitch and finally pull down at one corner. "It's not like I planned for it to happen. Hell, I don't even remember it."

"Oh, dear." Mother sighs. "Does your father know?"

I nod. "Of course he does. He thinks this is excellent leverage to have on Alexander."

We sit in silence for a few moments and then Mother says, "Maybe this isn't such a bad thing."

That's not exactly what I was expecting her to say. "How can you say that? Being married to Alexander King is one of the worst things I can ever imagine happening to me in my life."

"Are you sure about that?"

I push my half-eaten plate of food away before folding my arms across my chest. "Of course, I am. He's a pompous asshole, and I can't believe I allowed myself to get in to this situation."

"See, dear, that's where I think this marriage might not be such a bad thing."

Clearly, my mother is allowing Alexander's disgustingly good looks to blind her to the truth of how awful he is. "You're not grasping the—"

"I understand just fine." She cuts me off and then levels her gaze on me. "I'm not sure *you're* seeing that maybe fate has a way of intervening, even if you don't believe what's happening is the best thing. If you let your guard down enough to marry him, drunk or not, he can't be all bad, can he? There has to be some small part of you that enjoys being with him or else you would've never gone through with a quickie Vegas wedding."

I open my mouth to argue—to explain that the liquor completely impaired my judgment when it came to Alexander, but that wouldn't exactly be the truth. I had sex with the man two times before I even had a drink of alcohol. I have no excuse for that. Alexander King is a very intoxicating man, and it pisses me off that I find it so hard to resist him.

Chapter IV
HARD BALL

Margo

MY PALMS SWEAT AS I sit at my desk, waiting for the moment Alexander comes marching through the door. I don't recall the last time I've been this nervous. That man just has a way of pushing my buttons, even when he's not around. I seriously entertained Mom's idea of quitting, but I know Daddy would kill me if I gave up on saving the company, so here I am.

All night long, I ran scenarios through my head of what it would be like to see him today. I have loads of fiery dialogue just waiting to assault him the moment that cocky mouth of his opens and he says one cross thing to me.

The soft ding of the elevator stopping on this otherwise quiet floor catches my attention. I practically leap out of my seat, not wanting to be in a position to be talked down to if it is Alexander.

It's only seven. Most of the employees don't start rolling in for at least another forty-five minutes, but I know that

Alexander is always the first one at the office every morning.

I hold my breath as I hear heavy footsteps head in my direction.

Our gazes meet as soon as he rounds the corner and turns into my office. He's always so put together, and today is no different as he waltzes toward my desk in his perfectly pressed black suit. I stare into Alexander's gray eyes, ready to begin our verbal sparring match, but I never get the chance to say a word. He turns without so much as a word to me and storms into his adjoining office, slamming the door shut behind him in the process.

My mouth drops open. So much for my thought-out plan of attack.

I plop down in my chair and do my best to pretend the man, who is now my husband, isn't on the other side of that door, avoiding me at all costs.

Asshole.

I flip off the door but refuse to go chasing after him to demand answers. If he wants to play 'let's pretend last weekend never happened,' then so be it.

Game on.

He will not control my thoughts any longer. I won't allow it because I've done nothing but obsess about him since I arrived back in New York. If I haven't been daydreaming about the way his hands felt on me, then figuring out a way to take him down has consumed me. I wish he weren't such a fantastic lover. Maybe then, I could jerk my head out of the fucking clouds and stop thinking about Alexander King in toe-curling sexual positions.

I sigh and check the clock on my computer screen. It's nearly twelve, and there still hasn't been a peep out of Alexander. Not even for his coffee—which is odd since he always seems to take great pleasure in having me fetch on his command.

I'll be damned if I break the little silence game we have going on between us. I refuse to allow him to believe he has an inch of power over me. I still want him to think I'm ready to stick it to him at any moment for not having a prenup in place before he married me.

I return my attention back to the statistical figures for King Enterprises that I've been able to get my hands on. All morning, I've been looking for traces of unethical practices that can help me in my pursuit to take Alexander King down with a bit of blackmail. Unfortunately for me, nothing of use has turned up. To my surprise, this company seems to do everything by the book.

The phone on my desk rings, and I snatch it off my desk the moment Alexander's name flashes across the caller ID. "Yes, Mr. King. Is there something I can do for you?"

"I need a car brought around in exactly fifteen minutes," he orders without as much as a greeting.

I don't appreciate the bossy tone in his voice, so I decide to throw a little dig of my own at him. "Of course, sir. Is there anything else you need from me? Your messages, coffee, divorce papers? Oh, wait, I forgot that we need to tie up many loose ends before we close that deal."

The last one has me biting my lip to hold back a snicker. I don't even have to see the expression on his face to know that one has him seething.

"Margo . . ." he says my name with a warning, but I've decided I need to keep going—keep pushing his buttons.

"Do I detect some anger? Is that any way to speak to your wife? We are still in that newlywed phase, after all."

"Margo," he growls. "Get your ass in this office so we can discuss this matter privately. We don't need the entire fucking office knowing our goddamn business."

I raise my eyebrows while a smirk crosses my face. "No need to get touchy. I—"

Click.

Before I can throw out anything else, Alexander stops me in my tracks by hanging up.

The smile still rests on my face as I push myself up from my desk. I like the idea of having this egotistical man by the balls. His reputation of dicking women over precedes him in this city, so I love the idea that I've one-upped this man.

Now all I have to do is march in there and keep up this bitch persona. The only chance I have of keeping him at bay is to continue to piss him off. If he despises me, then he'll stay on the other side of that desk and not attempt to use those magical hands on me. Lord knows, if he touches me, I'll lose all self-control, and I cannot allow that to happen. This is my one shot at forcing Alexander King into not taking over my father's company. It's also one of my last chances to put distance between the two of us and regain control of my heart before it falls for this wicked man.

Chapter V
THE BARGAIN

Alexander

I ADJUST MY TIE FOR the third time and take a deep breath, readying myself to enter into battle with Margo. I hadn't planned her to be here early this morning, so when I walked in and saw her sitting at her desk, I froze and not one damn word would come out of my mouth. I figured silence was best until I could figure out a way to convince her of my plan. I spent some time last night figuring out how I could spin this situation to make me look good to the board.

The door swings open, and I lean back in my chair and steeple my fingers in front of me. If I've learned one thing about Margo, it's that she's a shark like me. Any sign of a little blood and she'll attack, so it's best to put on a good front and pretend that I'm not the least bit rattled.

Margo struts through the door with her chin tipped up, and I can tell by the heated expression on her face that getting her on my side will not be an easy task.

"Sit," I order her.

She shakes her head. "I think I'll stand."

Her little act of defiance doesn't surprise me. She hates being ordered around.

I want to lash out and say a million things that I know will get under her skin and piss her off even further, but I quickly think back to what Jack said. I have to stop fighting with this woman and get on her good side so she'll cooperate with not only the divorce process, but also with the other little plan that I have in mind.

I take a deep breath and push myself to be more pleasant with her. "Would you please have a seat, Margo?"

She arches one of her perfectly manicured eyebrows, clearly questioning my sudden manners. She stares me down a moment longer but then takes the seat across from me. Margo crosses those long, sexy legs of hers, and my eyes instantly dart down to them. She's wearing another one of those goddamn skirts that does nothing but accentuate every curve beneath it. A couple of buttons on her blue blouse are undone, the valley between her tits on display.

I pull at the collar of my shirt and do attempt to stop thinking about how fucking sexy she is both in and out of her clothes. "I have a proposition for you."

She narrows her eyes at me. "This had better not be another request to be your fuck buddy. The last time you propositioned me for that, I distinctly remember smacking your face."

My tongue dances behind my teeth, ready to remind her just how much she enjoyed having my cock buried inside her—how she begged for it. But I know doing that right now won't help my case.

"Look, Margo, you're an intelligent woman, so there's no need for me to beat around the bush. I need something from you."

This catches her interest, and both of her eyebrows shoot up. "And I suppose you believe I'll just give over whatever it is you need from me."

I lock my gaze with hers. "Yes."

She opens her mouth to protest, but I quickly cut her off.

"The answer is yes because I'm willing to make you a very generous offer."

She folds her arms over her chest. "What exactly is it that you want?"

"Your cooperation," I tell her honestly.

She smirks. "You want to divorce me so soon?"

"This isn't a joke, Margo. Our little moment of drunken indiscretion could put me in some deep shit."

"And this is my problem because . . . ?"

Her flippant attitude is really getting under my skin. "If you want to save your father's company, then it should matter to you if I'm no longer the one making final business decisions when it comes to the King Corporation."

She rolls those magnetic, blue eyes of hers. "You're really reaching, Alexander."

I pound my fist on my desk, causing her to jump and release a tiny gasp. "It's true, dammit."

Her eyes search my face as she chews on that plump bottom lip of hers, and then she asks softly, "How is that possible? I thought your father left you this company?"

"He did, but there is a catch. A clause written in his will states the board has the power to overthrow my position as president if it is deemed that I was making reckless decisions in either my professional or private life," I explain.

Her eyebrows draw in and there's a flash of pity in her eyes. "Why would he do that?"

"Because I was only nineteen years old when he was diagnosed with cancer and that's not exactly a mature age for a guy to run a Fortune 500 company without some protective measures in place." I shrug. "I understand why he did it. Hell, I would do the same thing in order to protect the family empire and make sure it remained profitable. He was looking out for my sister, Diem, and me."

Margo's lips twist. "But you're thirty years old now. Does that clause not have an expiration date?"

I nod. "It ends when I'm thirty-two. Father figured since that was the age he settled down, got married, and began building his empire that I should have my head on straight by then." I lean in and set my elbows on my desk. "That's why I need your cooperation. I need to convince the board that our marriage wasn't some random drunken act so they don't question my ability to run this company. I've worked my ass off since my father's death to prove not only to the board, but also to myself, that I'm fit to fill Father's shoes. I would want him to be proud of how well I've handled everything."

Silence settles in the office. I've never really admitted to anyone why I'm so driven, but it feels good to say it out loud. I just hope that Margo understands why this means so much to me and agrees to help me out.

Finally, after she's had time to process everything I've just told her, she launches into question mode. "So you're saying that you want to stay married and that you want me to play along and make the world believe that we're madly in love?"

"That's exactly what I'm asking."

Margo nods. "What's in it for me?"

I flinch. "I thought I was pretty clear about how me staying in power benefits you."

She shakes her head. "All you said was that if I wanted to save my father's business, then I would need to help you. I'm just sitting here asking myself why I would want to do that. I know your main objective is to buy out my father's entire company and then break it into pieces to sell off like it's some worn-out toy at a flea market."

I sigh, hating that what I'm about to propose goes against everything in me. "If you help me, then I promise that in return, I will not break apart your father's company and sell it off in sections as I originally planned. Instead, King Corporation will become a financial partner with Buchanan Industries. And as a bonus, I'll make sure Yamada Enterprises strikes up a deal with your father's company directly."

A wicked smile lights up Margo's face as she stands up and sticks her hand out to me. "You've got yourself a deal, baby."

Internally, I cringe, but I know I have to look at the bigger picture in this situation. Losing this deal with Buchanan Industries is going to hurt like a motherfucker, but losing control of my company will hurt a lot fucking worse.

I stand and then walk around the desk in order to take her hand in mine. Immediately, the warmth of her touch causes my heart to pound a little harder in my chest as my body craves to get my hands on more of her soft skin.

I lick my lips as my eyes flit down to her mouth. "I'll expect you to be at my house, suitcase in hand, by seven sharp."

"Excuse me?" Margo instantly attempts to pull away from my grasp, but I don't let her go. "You didn't say a thing about me living with you."

I cock my right eyebrow as I stare down at her. "Married couples generally live together."

"Yes, but typically those people like each other," she growls as she pulls again to break free of me.

A smirk crosses my face. "Are you saying that you don't like me?"

"I despise you," she hisses.

Whenever Margo gets into bitch mode, it triggers something in me that's so insanely attracted to her that I can barely contain myself. Before I even realize what I'm doing, I have her by the nape of the neck and am crushing my lips to hers.

At first her eyes widen, but she doesn't fight me a bit. As a matter of fact, it seems to turn her on. Because the next thing I know, her hands are in my hair and our bodies are pressed so close I can feel the curve of her tits against my chest.

I spin Margo around and push her ass against my desk. A loud crash echoes through the room as I shove all the paperwork from my desk to the floor.

I grip her hips as she shoves my jacket off my shoulders. "I've thought about fucking you on this desk since the first time I saw you." She moans into my mouth as I slide my hand between her thighs until my fingers trace the silky material of her panties. "I've missed the taste of this sweet pussy on my tongue. Just think about how fun this is going to be when we get to my apartment tonight."

I'm unable to resist the urge to touch her. She tosses her head back, and I seize the opportunity to nip at her earlobe and inhale her sweet perfume. My cock jerks inside my slacks, and I want nothing more than to take her right here. Right now.

I shove the silk material of her panties out of the way and slide my index finger against her swollen clit. "Always so wet, Margo. I love that about you."

With my free hand, I hitch her leg around my waist so I can spread her wide and work her into a frenzy.

"Oh, that's it," she moans as I continue my assault on her pussy. "Alexander . . ."

The way she says my name—all breathy while she's on the verge of orgasm—nearly makes me come in my pants. This woman has no idea how much she turns me on.

"Come for me, Margo," I order, needing to watch her as she lets go.

She lets out a cry that I'm sure the rest of the office would hear had she not buried her face into the crook of my neck. Her entire body shakes against me as I flick her click and she comes hard.

The heat of her breath warms the skin on my neck. Desperately needing my own release, I pull back and stare into her eyes. "Now, it's time for you to get on your knees for me."

As the words leave my mouth, a sharp pain slices through my bottom lip as Margo bites me just a little too hard. She shoves me away from her and then smacks me square in the face.

I rub my cheek, completely confused. "What the fuck was that for?"

Margo's nostrils flare as she draws back to smack me again. This time, I catch her by the wrist before she can make contact with my face. "Stop it! Jesus!"

She yanks her arm out of my grasp and straightens her skirt. "I don't like to be used. I thought I made it perfectly clear when we were in Vegas that I'm not going to be one of your hired hookers. If you think the deal we just made changes that, then you're sorely mistaken. Married or not, I am not some little slut for you to use whenever you feel like it."

She doesn't give me a chance to say another word. She turns on her heel and storms out of my door, slamming it so hard in the process that one of the pictures falls off the wall.

I stand there with my mouth agape like a fucking idiot. For once in my life, I'm at a fucking loss for words. The thought of using her in that manner never crossed my mind, but now that she's put it out there, having Margo Buchanan around as my live-in sex slave doesn't sound so bad.

Chapter VI
TWO'S COMPANY

Margo

AT SIX THIRTY ON THE dot, the car that Alexander promised has arrived to pick me up. On the way to his place gives me time to think. I honestly don't know how I'm going to survive living at his place. That man . . . he has a way of getting to me unlike any other person I have ever met. Every time he speaks to me, he evokes so many emotions within me. I have a hard time figuring out how to deal with them, considering my stupid body always seems to want to go against everything my highly educated brain is screaming not to do. I can't believe I kissed him.

I mean, what the hell was that in his office today, and why can't I stop liking it so much?

It's a horrible position to be in when you find your enemy insanely attractive.

The car comes to a stop, and the driver steps out of the car. This is it. No turning back now. I made a deal with a handsome as hell devil, and there's no going back.

I take a deep breath before I grab my purse and give myself a little pep talk. "You can do this. Be strong. And treat him like any other man whore who needs to be destroyed."

The driver opens the door and helps me out. I glance up at the towering building and stare for a moment at how impressive it is with its gleaming glass front. Leave it to King to own an apartment in one of the richest looking buildings in Lenox Hill.

"Good evening, Mrs. King. I've been expecting you." The voice laced with a heavy Scottish accent startles me, and I quickly refocus my gaze onto an older doorman with a friendly face. He smiles at me while his salt and pepper hair pokes out from under his hat. A few seconds pass and he tilts his head when I don't immediately respond, almost to question if I'm who he's been waiting for. "You are Mrs. King, correct?"

Hearing the name 'Mrs. King' throws me for a bit of a loop. It actually does take a second for it to register that I am, in fact, Mrs. Alexander King, and the whole purpose of me living here is to make people believe that we are indeed a married couple.

I clear my throat before I square my shoulders, reminding myself that I'm doing this to secure my rightful future and that I need to play my part in this whole happily-ever-after illusion. God knows I don't need to give Alexander any reason to argue with me. It seems that when we do that, we end up tearing at each other's clothes. "That's right. I believe my husband is expecting me."

This seems to satisfy the old man. He gives me a curt nod and then opens the door for me. "Right this way, Madame."

"Thank you . . ." I trail my words as I pass by him, unsure of his name.

"Darby," he announces while still wearing his smile.

I smile in return, completely at ease with this man who seems to be extremely friendly. I don't know how in the world the man keeps such a pleasant outlook considering he has one of the biggest pricks in Manhattan living in his place of employment. It's bad enough I have to fetch Alexander's coffee and whatever else he needs while being treated like crap. I can only imagine how unpleasant he must be toward Darby when he passes by him every day.

I make my way through the elegant lobby and listen to the heels of my shoes click on the marble tile as I head toward the elevator. When I press the up button, it occurs to me that I have no clue what floor Alexander's apartment is on.

I turn toward the front door where Darby busies himself collecting my bags from the driver and placing them on a gold plated trolley. I bite my lip, unease suddenly rocking through me at the realization of how unprepared I am for this situation.

The panic I feel must be evident on my face because the moment the doorman pushes his cart up next to me, he asks, "Are you all right, Madame?"

I tuck a loose strand of my dark hair back behind my ear. "Oh, yes. I'm perfectly fine."

Darby's quiet for a few moments. "You know, I was a wee bit nervous the first night my bonny lass and I settled into our cottage together. I believe that's normal for everyone when they get married."

"Oh, I'm not—" The elevator dings cutting me off before I babble on how I'm not going out of my mind right now when, in fact, I am.

I step inside and move to the side so Darby can squeeze inside with my things.

Darby punches the 'P' button on the elevator, so I make a mental note to remember that for next time. "I don't think you'll have anything to worry about. Alex is a good lad."

I bunch my brow together. Since I've met Alexander King, I've never heard anyone address him so informally, so this takes me aback and makes me a bit curious. "Have you worked for Alexander long?"

Darby nods. "Aye. The missus and me have worked for Alex's family for the better part of thirty years now—since Alex was a wee babe. I think that's about the time we moved to the States from Ottawa Valley. Aggie practically raised Alex and Diem, you know."

That's a lot of information to take in, but one thing definitely stood out to me about that story. "So when you say that you've worked for his family . . . do you mean that the Kings own this building?"

"Aye," he answers. "It's been in the King family for generations. When Alexander's father inherited it, he decided to turn the penthouse into his family home."

From the research I had done on Alexander, I discovered that his father was a very family-oriented man with a reputation of integrity. It was clear by all the photos I found of the two of them before Mr. King had passed away that Alexander and his father were close. So it doesn't exactly surprise me that this building, much like his company, was passed on to his son too.

When the elevator's doors open into the hall, only one door comes into view. It's painted a soft cream color and trimmed in gold accents, making it very reminiscent of a much more regal era when paired with the red carpet that also contain gold trim. Just to the right of the door is a small box that appears to be an intercom. I stand back as Darby presses the call button to alert a bell on the other side of the door.

"Yes?" an older lady's voice calls over the box.

"Aggie, I've got the new Mrs. King for ye. Care to open the door and let the lass inside?"

Within moments, the locks on the other side of the door jingle, and the door is opened, revealing a foyer fit for a palace. My eyes widen at the sight of all the marble with gold accents. A staircase stands proudly in the middle of the space, leading up to another level of the apartment. This entry takes me back to a time when I was a little girl and dreamed of being a princess living in a castle; only it's more amazing than my dreams.

"Don't be shy. Come on in." The lady who I'm banking is Aggie, Darby's wife, holds the door open for me.

She smiles as I pass her, and much like her husband, there's a very friendly energy surrounding Aggie. The blue of her maid's uniform enriches the color of her ocean-blue eyes while her gray hair sits in a low bun, showing off her round face.

Darby follows me inside, and Aggie quickly turns her attention from me to her husband. "He's done well, hasn't he, Darby? This one is a pretty one."

A blush creeps over my cheeks as I listen to the woman dote on me.

Aggie closes the door, causing the bottom hem of her uniform to swish about a bit. "Now that we're alone, we want you to know that Darby and myself know the truth about the situation at hand, so there'll be no need in puttin' on a show fur the likes of us."

I raise my eyebrows, still not sure if I should break my cover just in case they really don't know that Alexander and I didn't really mean to get married.

"Don't look so surprised, dear. There's not much that Alex keeps from us. He gave us all the details. I still can't believe that Henry put that silly clause in his will. I tried to explain that just because he was wild until he was thirty-two didn't mean that our Alex would be the same. I wish Henry were here to see just how well his son has done with running the empire he built. He would've been so proud and that little clause would never have existed." Aggie sighs. "It's just a shame Alex still has to deal with all this." She quickly backpedals. "Not that it's anything to do with you personally, dear. I'm sure you're a lovely young lady and we'll be happy to have ye here until this mess is settled. I just wish he didn't have to go through proving that he's capable of running a business even though he makes a few mistakes."

"The lad is only human," Darby chimes in. "Can't expect him to be perfect all the time."

"He's far from perfect." My eyes widen the moment I realize that I've actually said what was running through my mind. Not wanting to offend two people who clearly care for Alexander, I try to correct my mistake. "Er—I mean . . ."

Darby laughs. "No wonder he likes her. She's a feisty one."

Aggie nods in agreement. "Aye. Maybe he's found his match."

I stand there, completely unsure of what to say.

"Come on, lass. Let me show yew to where you'll be staying," Aggie instructs and then turns toward the staircase. "Darby will bring your bags up to your room. I'm sure you'll need to freshen up for dinner."

Once at the top of the stairs, Aggie leads me down a wide hallway lined with paintings. Some of the paintings are abstract pieces, while a few focus on people. Each one is more beautiful than the last. One, in particular, catches my attention.

It's Alexander.

He sits in a high-back leather chair, and the dark background causes the red tie he's wearing to pop out against his gray suit. It's uncanny how lifelike the piece looks. There's a hint of mischief in his gray eyes paired with that signature cocky grin.

Even in a painting Alexander King appears to be up to no good. It's amazing how even a picture of him causes my body to do crazy things, like yearn his touch.

"These are beautiful," I tell Aggie, who's waiting patiently for me to study the pictures that I'm sure she's passed by a million times. "Are they all the same artist?"

"They are." Alexander's voice causes me to jump.

Clearly, I wasn't expecting him to be the one to answer me.

My back goes ramrod straight with the arrival of the unwelcome asshole who owns the place. The relaxed mood that Aggie and Darby had created the moment I stepped foot inside this building is suddenly gone.

Alexander comes strutting down the hall, wearing a white oxford rolled up to his elbows and the same dark slacks he had on earlier in the office. He's clearly made himself more comfortable since the last time I'd seen him today.

He stops about a foot away and then turns to stare at the portrait of himself. "It's a great likeness, don't you think? I look pretty damn fantastic, if you ask me."

I have to fight the urge to roll my eyes at his outward show of cockiness. "It's very nice work. It's too bad the artist didn't have a better subject. If they'd had someone different, then perhaps this would be in a museum somewhere."

A hint of a smile crosses his lips. "Margo, you have an uncanny ability to insult me and yet throw out a compliment. In this case, I'll allow your snide jab at me to slide, considering you've just praised my little sister's work."

"Diem did this?" I raise my eyebrows, and it hits me instantly that I remember his sister from high school. Even back then, she was an artist, which made her stand out from all the other kids, and that's how I remember her. Most kids I went to school with were obsessed with getting into top-notch colleges in order to be able to work for their family businesses, but not Diem. She was all about art and expressing herself.

He motions to the other paintings hanging on both sides of the hall. "She did all of these. She very passionate about her work, and she actually just sold her first piece shortly before we left for Las Vegas."

"That's fantastic," I answer honestly. "She's clearly very talented."

This time when he smiles, it's more reminiscent of a proud parent. It's nice to know he's not a heartless jackass in all facets of his life.

"Come," Alexander instructs. "I'll show you to your room."

He turns to go back the way he came down the hall, and I follow, suddenly aware that Aggie is no longer with us.

We pass a couple of doors. Alexander explains that one is a bathroom and that there are seven in total in the apartment. The second door belongs to his little sister who still stays with him from time to time.

"I take it that the two of you get along well," I state as we pass by Diem's room.

He shrugs. "For the most part, we do. There are times when she tries my patience, but I guess that's what little sisters do."

"Does your mother still have to break up fights between the two of you like she did when you were children?"

This question causes Alexander's body to stiffen. "My mother hasn't been in our lives for quite some time."

"I'm sorry to hear that," I tell him as the feeling of pity for the loss of a mother wafts over me. Nowhere in my research about Alexander King did it talk about a strained relationship with his mother. It then falls upon me to lighten the mood since I seemed to have brought up a touchy subject. "Well, seems to be her loss, and Diem seems to be able to create in spite of her not being around."

He nods but doesn't say another word about the topic.

Clearly talking about his mother isn't something that he likes to do. I make a mental note about that so I tread lightly on the subject stay on his good side. I want this little arrangement to go off without a hitch. In order for the board to believe that we're a happy couple, we have to maintain what I like to refer to as a pleasant working relationship.

When we come to the third door on the left, Alexander stops. "This is your room. You may decorate it however you wish while you're here. If you need anything at all, please feel free to ask Aggie or Darby. They will see to your needs. Unless your needs are of the sexual variety. In that case, I expect you to report directly to me so that I can assist you with that. I like for all my guests to be satisfied."

"And there's the asshole I know," I say. "I wondered where you'd been hiding for the last few minutes."

Alexander pulls a key from his pants pocket and then dangles it in front of me. "You know very well that I can be *nice* when I want to be, Margo. I thought I was very accommodating in Vegas."

There's no mistaking the teasing tone of his voice, and it pisses me off. I don't like the fact that I gave in to this man, and I don't like him throwing the fact that I've fucked him in my face. And I for damn sure want to make sure that he knows that he's never getting inside these panties ever again.

I narrow my eyes. "Well, don't worry about being nice to me while I'm here. I made sure to pack my own battery-powered happiness maker, so I'm afraid I won't need you to accommodate anything relating to me ever again."

That trademark grin returns in full force. "I seem to remember you making these same threats before, and we still ended up married."

"For now," I reply and then snatch the key from his hand. "That's one problem I intend to remedy as soon as possible."

He leans against the wall and folds his arms over his chest. "Well, Princess, I hate to be the one to burst whatever perfectly planned little bubble you've got going on in that beautiful brain of yours, but we're not separating until I'm sure the board buys that we were at least madly in love when we said I do and we have to pay Yamada a visit on his island this coming Thurday."

I twist my lips. I wish I could go back and punch myself square in the face during that part of our nuptials and scream 'I don't!' because now King has me by the proverbial balls, and he knows it. I just have to keep cool and not lose my head, even though the man is frustratingly gorgeous and has a body that I wouldn't mind seeing naked again. Being so attracted to him complicates the hell out of things.

I will not be lured into temptation. I still have a job to do. Winning back Buchanan Industries and securing my future must be my main focus. It's time to keep my eyes on the prize and not on Alexander's stunning physique or his promises of naughty pleasure.

"Don't worry, King. This marriage is nothing more than a business relationship for me. I'll uphold my end of the deal. By the time I'm through putting on a show, this whole damn town will believe that we're the most in love couple on the planet." I square my shoulders after my little mental pep talk and shove the key into the door. I pass Alexander and step into the room without saying another word.

Chapter VII
SHOCK AND AWE

Alexander

MARGO DIDN'T COME OUT OF her room at all last night. Aggie got worried after a while and checked on her, but she still couldn't convince her to come down to the main floor of the apartment for dinner. Instead, Aggie fixed a tray and took it up to her. She told me that I needed to give the girl time to adjust to the situation and reminded me that I'm not always the easiest man to live with.

This morning, I got the same coldness from Margo when I offered her a ride to work. I explained that it would be best to be seen coming to the office together since we're a happily married couple.

I could tell that she was reluctant, but she agreed.

I steal a quick glance in her direction in the elevator. Her dark hair is down today, flowing freely in big waves over her shoulders. It's such a stark contrast from the bright red dress she's wearing that I can't help but notice every curve on her body.

As if she can feel my eyes studying the contours of her body, she turns her head and points her gaze right at me. I don't make any apologies when she catches me either. I never say sorry unless I mean it, and in this case, I don't think there's anything wrong with staring at the work of art that's Margo's body. So I might as well compliment her on it.

"Your tits look amazing in that dress. You should wear it more often," I tell her.

She narrows her eyes. "Do you always have to be so crass?"

"Yes," I muse with a smile. "It's part of my charm."

"Who said you were charming?" she jabs back at me.

I raise one eyebrow. "I seem to recall being able to charm you out of your panties on more than two occasions."

"Well," she scoffs. "Everyone loses their mind from time to time. If anyone ever questions me about it, I'll plead temporary insanity."

"Insane with lust, you mean." I chuckle.

"Hardly," she says as the elevator doors open.

When we step out into the lobby, Darby stands near the front exit. He smiles the moment his eyes land on us. I know what he's thinking. God knows he and Aggie have voiced how beautiful Margo is enough times since they met her yesterday. Although they aren't entirely pleased with the way I ended up married, they somehow believe Margo might be a suitable match for me since she doesn't seem to take my shit. While their opinions mean a great deal to me because I consider them to be my family, I don't think they know what in the hell they're talking about. They obviously don't know the bitchy side of Margo like I do. Once they see that come out, I'm sure they'll be celebrating the day I get Margo to sign the divorce papers.

Without permission, I wrap my arm around Margo's waist and pull her tightly against me.

She begins to pull away nearly instantly. "What in the hell do you think you're doing?"

"Acting married and madly in love, of course," I reply as smoothly as I can.

She shakes her head. "There's no one here to put on a show for."

I swirl my index finger in a circle. "There are eyes everywhere. If we want to be believed, anytime we're in public we need to make our relationship appear to be real. So get ready because these hands will be on you a lot."

I can tell by the heated expression on Margo's face that she would love nothing more than to smack my hand away. The woman seems to be very fond of inflicting pain to my face with her hands. I can tell this is killing her to allow me to grope her a little in public, but before she has time to argue much more, Darby steps in front of us to open the door.

"It's almost working," Darby says. "The two of you aren't smiling. If you want the world to buy it, you'll be needin' to sell it a wee bit more."

I glance down at Margo and plaster on the biggest grin that I can fit on my face. "Hear that, sweetie. We both need to smile. We're in love, remember?"

"How can I forget," she replies with a dry tone. "How's this?"

She tips her head and stares up at me, and it gives me a moment to stare into those gorgeous blue eyes of hers. The moment she smiles, I swear to God my breath catches. I've never believed in the saying 'You take my breath away,' but it just fucking happened to me.

"You're perfect," I tell her, and at that moment, I mean it.

My honesty must surprise her because her usual sarcastic comment doesn't follow. Instead, her eyes remain locked on mine as she swallows hard.

My heart is pounding like a thoroughbred's hooves beating against the ground. I know it makes me sound like a complete fucking pussy, but if I had met Margo Buchanan in a different way, I could see myself actually being with this woman. Not only is she the hottest thing I've ever seen, but she's wicked smart and has a witty tongue. Beauty and brains like hers are a rarity. She's like finding a goddamn unicorn.

Darby clears his throat. "Your car has arrived, Alex."

I shake my head, breaking out of my daze. I can't seem to keep my head on straight when I'm with Margo, and I need to figure out a way to stop that. So much is riding on every move I make right now. I can't afford to screw anything up. My head has to be in the game at all times, or I might lose everything.

The car ride to the office is quiet. I'm sure we both have a lot of thinking to do and neither of us find it necessary to make small talk. I appreciate the silence.

When we step into the elevator to head up to the office, I tell her, "Even though this is a work setting, we still need to maintain our little act, so I expect you to play your part of doting wife."

Margo smoothes her hair down with her fingers. "Don't worry, King. I know my part and I plan to play it well, so you better hold up your end of the deal."

"I never go back on my word."

"Good to know," she says.

The elevator dings, and as if on cue, I place my hand on the small of her back. Her body shivers under my touch, and I fight back a smirk. It pleases me greatly to know that I have that effect on her.

The doors open, and since I'm much later than normal, every set of eyes in the front office is on us the instant we walk in together.

Margo stiffens, and I know she'll probably hate what I'm about to do, but I want everything out in the open as quickly as possible. I'm the kind of man who wants to break the bad news to the world instead of allowing speculation to run wild.

I lean down and kiss her cheek and then whisper, "It's best to maintain control at all times, don't you agree?"

She nods and then pulls back and smiles. "Absolutely."

That's when she does something that shocks the shit out of me. She traces my cheek with the tips of her fingers before she kisses me. I close my eyes briefly and allow myself the pleasure of tasting her lips. She's so damn addictive.

She pulls away before I'm ready, but I know it would be definitely crossing the line to fuck her in front of an audience even though my cock is growing stiff in my slacks. That's a sexual harassment lawsuit just waiting to happen.

Margo saunters away, giving her hips an extra swish as she heads toward her desk, and it causes me to smile. That naughty little minx knows how to play her part very well indeed. Hell, if she keeps that up, *I* might just begin to buy into it.

It's unusually quiet in the office, and I turn my attention back to the front office staff who are all frozen in place with their mouths agape. That's enough of a show for them.

"What are you all looking at? Back to work," I order, and they all instantly go back to pretending to be in a huge rush.

I stalk past them all, and then come to a halt when I find myself at Margo's desk. "Good work, Mrs. King."

She smiles. "Let me know if they need an encore to buy it."

I shake my head before turning toward my office. "I think we've stunned them enough for one day."

I try to stay busy for the rest of the day by finalizing a few small deals I've been working on. When it's nearly lunchtime, there's a quick knock on my door before Jack comes striding in.

He has a huge grin on his face, so I know that he's pleased to hear that people are buying into the little act with Margo. "You son-of-a-bitch. You've done it. People actually believe that you and Margo are in love. I never thought you'd be able to get her to go along with it."

I lean back in my chair and my lips pull up at one corner. "Come on, Jack. You're acting like you've just met me. You know I can close any deal. This thing with Margo is nothing but another deal."

He plops down in the chair in front my desk. "So if this is just a deal, it means that you've promised her something."

This was the part of my plan that I dreaded explaining to Jack, but I knew it had to be done. I stand up and then smooth my tie down before heading over to the bar. I flip two glasses over and pull the glass cork from the crystal decanter before pouring the scotch.

"Shit," Jack mutters as he pushes himself up from the chair. "If you're pouring the liquor before one, I know you're about to break some bad news to me. Please tell me that you didn't give in to her demands and promise her something completely unreasonable."

I sigh and hand him a glass. "What would you have me do, Jack? I can't very well lose control of my father's company."

He shakes his head. "I get that, man. I do. But couldn't you figure out something else to give her—write her a check or something? We'll lose so much money if this Buchanan deal doesn't go through."

As much as it pains me to think about walking away from the deal I've been working on for months and losing out on all the money that we stand to make, it hurts way fucking worse to think about a bunch of old, greedy bastards running the company that my father built.

Chapter VIII
PUPPY LOVE

Margo

THE FIRST DAY WE WENT public was the hardest. Since then, rumors have been flying all around the city. Gossip in this town spreads at lightning speed, especially when it involves the Naughty King and the Feisty Princess *willingly* committing to each other. If I were on the receiving end of that news, I would pity the idiots for thinking a relationship like that can actually work.

Good thing I'm not in this relationship for something as silly as love.

I don't believe in love. I've seen too much when it comes to relationships; not only courtesy of my mother, but also from the assholes I've dated. One, in particular, did a number on my heart, so I learned that in order to not get hurt, you have to keep your feelings on a tight leash at all times.

At this point, I couldn't care less if people pity me and think I'm a dumb twit who Alexander will blindside. I'm doing this for me and the company that will rightfully belong to me someday.

I find myself curled up on a chaise lounge in one of the biggest private libraries I've ever seen. Ever since I was a little girl, I've enjoyed reading. Sneaking my mother's romance novels and reading them in secret was one of my favorite pastimes. I find that as an adult, whenever I'm feeling stressed, a steamy romance seems to take my mind off reality for a bit. And this feels like the perfect place to hide out other than my room while I'm trapped here.

"Alexander? Aggie?" I hear a female voice call from the front of the apartment. "Anyone here?"

The distinct sound of heels clicking against the marble alerts me that whoever is in here is heading my way. I slide a bookmark into place and then swing my legs over the side of the seat just in time to see a four-legged ball of fur bound in my direction.

The yellow lab pup jumps into my lap and instantly assaults my face with his wet tongue. I giggle as I try to pull him off me. "My, you're a friendly thing, aren't you?" As if to answer me, the puppy barks and then places a paw on my arm. I stroke his head and smile. "You're about the cutest thing I've seen in a long time."

"Jimmy Chew!" The voice from earlier sounds in the room I'm in. "There you are!" The moment my eyes land on the woman, I instantly remember her from high school. Diem looks exactly the same, with her long blond hair and bright green eyes, only now she's a little older and more beautiful.

Diem rushes over to me. "I'm so sorry, Margo. Jimmy is obviously still in need of a few lessons with a good obedience trainer."

I wave her off, surprised that she remembers me as well. "It's no problem at all. I actually love dogs."

She smiles. "Me, too."

"His name is cute," I tell her as I continue to pet Jimmy.

Diem sits on the couch across from me on the other side of the large wooden coffee table. "Thanks. Those are my favorite shoes, so when I was thinking about a name, that was the first thing that popped into my mind."

"I think it's an excellent choice." I glance in her direction and feel the need to strike up a conversation so we're not sitting here in awkward silence. "I was admiring your paintings the other day. They are quite good."

Her smile widens. "That's very kind of you. Thank you. I actually just sold my very first piece, so I'm hopeful that's a testament to my having true talent."

"Congratulations. Alexander told me that the other evening."

Diem adjusts on the couch, and I can tell by the way she's fidgeting in the seat that she's uncomfortable. She's probably wondering what in the hell I'm doing in her family home considering we never really spoke back in school.

She licks her lips and eyes me suspiciously. "So it's true, then—the rumors about you and my brother being married?"

Looks like she knows exactly why I'm here. Word travels quickly in this city.

It shouldn't shock me that Alexander didn't tell his sister. I mean, after all, he didn't mean to marry me or make me apart of his family, so I can see why he wouldn't want his sister in all this. But it still doesn't mean it was the right thing to do. If he wants people to believe that we are actually married, then he should've told his family, just as I told mine.

My lips pull into a tight line. Confirming this for Diem might piss Alexander off, but it has to be done.

"It's true," I say with ease that surprises me.

Diem tilts her head. "That must've been some trip to Vegas. I'm betting that Yamada was involved in some way."

I nod. "I'm not positive because the details are all still a little fuzzy, but I think he was the ringleader of the whole thing."

"I knew it!" she exclaims. "Honestly, I'm shocked. I was afraid the two of you would kill each other in Vegas. Never in my wildest dreams did I ever imagine this happening, but I should've expected it. Whenever Alexander and Yamada get together, something crazy always happens."

"They seem like quite the pair."

"That's putting it lightly." She chuckles. "The two alone are something, but when you add Jack to the mix, scandalous debauchery ensues. The three of them together is like one big fat never-ending party."

"I can see that. Jack and Alexander seem a lot alike," I tell her.

"You know, I used to think that too, but Jack has really shown me a different side of himself lately. He can be a gentleman when he wants to be." A slight blush creeps into her cheeks, and I instantly wonder if Diem has a crush on her brother's best friend. "He's actually the person to whom I sold my first painting."

I lift my eyebrows. "Wow. That's awesome. I didn't take Jack as an art buff, but I'm sure the painting he bought was stunning just like the rest of your work displayed around here."

"You really are too kind, but I don't know if I would necessarily refer to the piece that he bought as beautiful considering it was a self-portrait."

"Really?" Now that adds a twist to this little story. Maybe the attraction is a mutual thing. I bet Alexander doesn't have the first clue that his little sister and his best friend seem to be into one another. "Well, it sounds to me like Jack digs the woman who painted it a lot." I give her a wink.

Her blush colors her cheeks in full force as she lifts her shoulders in a bashful shrug. "I'm still not sure about that yet, and he hasn't made any real moves yet, but I think it's because he's afraid of what Alexander might say."

"Who's afraid of me now?" Alexander's voice slices through the room, and Diem instantly stiffens.

Alexander struts into the room and stops directly in front of me, folding his arms across his broad chest. Diem's back is to him, and she's staring at me with wide-eyes, begging me silently not to say a word about what she just admitted to me.

His eyes flick down to Jimmy, who is now asleep on my lap. "I wasn't aware that you had a dog."

"Oh, he's—"

"That's because he's not Margo's dog." Before I have a chance to stumble over explaining that the cute little pup isn't mine, Diem feels the need to interject. Diem turns toward her brother. "That's what we were just talking about, actually. I was afraid of what you would say about the dog."

Alexander sighs. "You have your own apartment, Squirt. If you want a dog to keep you company, you don't have to ask my permission. You're the one who'll have to take responsibility for it."

"The thing is, the dog isn't actually for me either. He's for you."

Alexander furrows his brow. "Why would you get me a dog?"

Diem stands up, and the moment she does, Jimmy's little head pops up to watch her. She steps over to me and scoops the dog up into her arms. "I actually picked him out weeks ago before he was weaned from his mother. I thought a dog might keep you company since I moved out. If I had known you were about to get married, I might have reconsidered buying you the dog."

Alexander's eyes flick in my direction, and I instantly throw my hands up in surrender. "Don't look at me. She knew before she got here."

His gaze shoots back over to Diem. "How?"

She chews on the corner of her lower lip. "Everyone's buzzing about it. It seems that the two of you kissed in front of the entire staff of King, and they started researching the shit out of the two of you. They found notice of your marriage license online somehow."

"Shit," he growls before scrubbing his hand down his face.

"Here," she says as she places Jimmy in Alexander's arms. "They say dogs relieve stress."

"Diem . . . no . . . I don't need a dog." Alexander stands there stiffly, cradling the yellow pup in his arms.

Diem turns and sits back down. "I dare you to resist that face. His name is Jimmy

Chew and he's the most adorable thing on this entire planet."

He stares down at the tiny ball of fur. Jimmy stretches his neck in order to lick Alexander's face, which causes him to smile. "He *is* pretty cute."

Diem lets out a little squeal. "See! I knew even you wouldn't be immune."

I catch myself grinning from ear to ear at the very sight of Alexander holding what quite possibly may be the most adorable puppy on the planet. It allows me to see another glimpse of that easygoing guy I spotted with Yamada the night of Yamada's party in Vegas—the guy he likes to keep hidden from me and the rest of the world.

"You didn't want people to know that the two of you were married?" Diem questions with a confused expression as she watches Alexander cradle Jimmy in his arms. "If that's the case, then you probably shouldn't have made out in front of fifty people."

"It wasn't fifty," he refutes instantly.

"Same difference," she counters. "What's the big deal? You meant to get married, right?" Alexander sighs as he takes a seat next to her. She tilts her head and studies her brother. "You didn't, did you?"

King's lips pull into a tight line and then his eyes flick to mine quickly before he turns his gaze to Diem. "No."

My mouth drops open. I can't believe he just exposed the secret he's been hell-bent on keeping. I'm tempted to say something, but stop myself, knowing that it's his secret. If he trusts his sister with it, that's his business. I just hope she doesn't go blabbing about it to the rest of the city.

"Yamada?" She only has to say his name like a question, and it seems to resonate with Alexander.

He nods. "Yes. And now it's a fucked-up mess. The board will be all over my ass because of that stupid clause Father put in his will if it gets out that Margo and I rushed into this unintentionally. Jack is afraid the board will see it as a weakness, accompanied by poor decision-making, and swoop in to contest my sole authority to make decisions for the King Corporation."

Diem's mouth drops open. "They can't do that, can they?"

"Afraid so, but Margo has agreed to help me convince everyone that we're a happily married couple."

Diem turns her attention to me. "That's really awesome of you, considering I know the two of you don't really get along so well."

I open my mouth to reply, but Alexander cuts me off.

"Don't toot her horn too much, Squirt. It's not like she's doing this out of the goodness of her heart. She's getting something out of it too."

"Just what's rightly mine and you know it," I fire back in my defense.

She lifts her eyebrows. "Oh? Well, I'm still glad she's doing it. I don't want you to have any issues with Daddy's company. I knew it meant a lot that it would be in your hands when he was no longer here. And on that note—" Diem pushes herself up from the couch. "I'd better get going so you two can get ready."

"Ready?" I asked confused as to what she's referring to.

"For the King Corporation Education Gala, of course. It's the company's biggest event of the year, and they will expect Alexander to make an appearance with his new bride. If you ask me, it's the perfect time to convince the board that you're a happy couple."

"You're right," Alexander says as he stands. "I hadn't told Margo because I didn't think it would be a good idea to have her there, but it might be best to confront the board head-on before the rumors get to them. Here." He begins to hand Jimmy back to Diem, but she shakes her head. "Come on. What am I supposed to do with him?"

Diem smiles and begins to backpedal out of the room. "He's your dog. You'll figure it out. Good luck, you two."

Once she leaves the room, Alexander turns to me. "The gala begins at eight. I know it doesn't leave you much time to get ready, but there are new gowns in your closet that will fit the occasion. I had Aggie pick up a few for you just in case I needed you to accompany me to the gala. Choose whichever one you like."

As much as I want to argue and tell him that I'm not going, I know that in order to uphold my end of the deal, I need to play my part. A wife would be happy to attend something like this on husband's arm, so I'll have to force myself to smile.

I push up from the chaise. "I'll be ready."

Alexander nods. "Thank you." As if on cue, Jimmy barks. "I can't believe she got me a dog. She knows how busy I am."

I smile as I lean in and pet the dog. "I think it's sweet that she cares enough about you to worry about you being lonely."

Alexander's gaze locks on mine the moment I glance up at his face. He opens his mouth to say something as his eyes search my face, and this weird tension floats between us. I'm not sure what he was about to say to me, but whatever it is, he's holding back.

I'm curious as to what it might've been, but I don't ask. Instead, I step around him and head toward my room. "I'll meet you in the foyer?"

"Seven thirty sharp," he calls over his shoulder.

As I head to my room, it hits me that living in this apartment with Alexander King hasn't been anything like I expected. Everything from his relationship with Aggie and Darby to his willingness to give in to his sister has all surprised me. Maybe there is some truth to what Yamada was saying about Alexander having a heart because I'm pretty sure I just caught a glimpse of it back there.

Chapter IX
THE GAME PLAN

Alexander

STANDING IN THE FOYER OF my apartment, I glance down at my watch. What in the hell takes a woman so damn long to get ready?

Jimmy paws at my leg, begging for my attention. I bend down and scratch the soft fur behind his right ear. "I can't play right now, buddy. You be good for Aggie while I'm gone."

Diem's right. I have a hard time resisting this dog no matter how hard I try.

A sigh escapes me as I stand upright and check my watch *again*. I hate being late; it's a pet peeve of mine. I always have to be early. I'm tempted to go to Margo's room to tell her to hurry her sweet ass up, but before I can decide, she appears at the top of the staircase.

My breath catches at the very sight of her in her black gown. She pauses for a brief second, and our eyes meet just before she descends the staircase. It's like watching a scene from a movie with her moving in slow motion, as she gets closer and closer to me. She's pulled her dark hair back, and the style accentuates her gorgeous face. She's even more stunning than any time I've ever seen her before. It's truly like staring at a piece of art, but I don't think Diem could even create something so perfect. I can't pull my eyes away.

I stand there with my mouth hanging open, and it's hard for me to even find the appropriate words to say to her as she halts directly in front of me.

Margo glances down at her outfit and runs her hand over her stomach as if to smooth out the fabric that's already lying perfectly in place. "It doesn't fit exactly right, but I think it can work for a few hours."

I bite my bottom lip. "You're stunning, Margo."

Her hypnotic blue eyes flit up to meet mine, and my heart flutters in my chest. "Thank you. That's the first real compliment you've ever given me."

I tilt my head. "I don't believe that's true. I distinctly remember telling you that you had great tits."

She bends down to pet Jimmy on the top of his head before flicking her eyes back in my direction. "Why do you always do that?"

"Do what?" I ask, completely perplexed as to what she's referring to.

"Get crude with me every time we have a conversation. Every time you say something sweet to me, I almost start believing you aren't a complete asshole, but you always ruin the moment with that mouth of yours. It wouldn't kill you to be nice every once in a while."

Her words stun me for a moment. I didn't mean to insult her, and having her in a pissy mood before we leave for this event isn't ideal. God knows I don't need her bitching me out in front of the very people who need to believe we're in a real relationship.

"You're right, Margo. I'll work on that," I tell her. "I promise to tone things down a bit."

"Thank you," she replies. "It will be nice not to be sexually harassed by you every time we have a conversation."

"I'm not saying it'll never happen again. I mean, have you seen you? I can't help thinking about your body and sex when I see you. You're sexy as hell," I admit.

Redness creeps up into her cheeks, and it's the first time anything I've ever said to her has caused that reaction. At that very moment, I realize the way to win Margo Buchanan over is with flattery. My habitual filthy talk had turned her on and helped me find my way into that sweet pussy of hers, but it never made her blush. It was like it pissed her off, but she was so turned on that she allowed me to fuck her even against her better judgment. But telling her how amazing I think she looks and meaning it affects her.

"Ready?" she prompts.

I shake my head. My palms begin to sweat as I reach into the pocket of my dress slacks. The velvet box in my hand suddenly feels like it weighs a ton as I hold it out to her. "I got you something."

Her eyes widen. "Alexander . . ."

"It's just a replacement for the one I gave you in Vegas. If we are going to pull this off, then we need to pull out all the stops and make our relationship believable. If you were really my wife, the ring on your finger would be large enough for the entire world to see. I would want everyone to know that you were mine. Clearly, our options in Vegas were limited when we went ring shopping in the middle of the night."

I open the black velvet lid, revealing the fifteen-carat diamond ring that I bought her from *Jacob and Co.*

Margo gasps as her hand flies to cover her mouth. "Oh, my God. Alexander! I cannot accept that."

I pull it out of the box and hold it out to her. "Consider it a thank-you gift for helping me. It's yours to keep, and you may do as you please with it once we're through with this whole marriage thing."

I wait with bated breath for her answer. She stares down at it, and for a moment it almost feels like I'm actually proposing to her. "What do you say, Margo? Will you be my fake wife?"

"Yes," her answer comes out barely above a whisper and relief floods through me.

I would've felt like a complete jackass for getting a replacement ring if she would've ended up saying no.

She swallows hard as she takes the ring from me. "It's the most gorgeous thing I've ever seen."

"Allow me." I snap the box closed and stuff it back into my pocket before taking the ring and sliding it onto Margo's ring finger. I stare down at her hand, memorized by the way it sparkles. It actually looks even better than I expected on her.

"It's perfect," she says. "I love it. Thank you, Alexander."

I turn and then extend my right elbow to her. "Come on, Mrs. King. It's time to break every woman's heart in Manhattan."

She shakes her head as she loops her arm through mine. "You are so damn full of yourself."

I shrug while wearing a lopsided grin. "It's not being conceited when it's the truth. You know as well as I do that most of the women in this city dream about taming me. They'll be jealous as hell once they see for themselves that you've hooked me."

"So you think I'm about to walk into a pissed off beehive because you're off the market?"

I nod. "I hope you're prepared to use that witty tongue of yours to ward off all the questions you're about to be bombarded with. I need you to defend our relationship to anyone who questions it. It's vital that you're in on this charade with me one hundred percent."

She pats my forearm with her other hand as if to soothe me. "Don't worry. We've got this."

I stare down at her and smile. "Shall we?"

With that, we say our goodbyes to Jimmy and head toward the front door. I take a deep breath and mentally prepare myself for what I'm sure is about to be a very interesting evening.

Chapter X
HELL OF A RIDE

Margo

IT'S A QUICK RIDE TO the gala or at least it felt that way. Alexander and I spent the time going over scenarios of what we would say to members of the board once we ran into them at the event. If there's one thing I can say about Alexander King, it's that he likes to be thorough.

We're sitting in the back of the limo, waiting for our turn to be dropped off at the entrance, when Alexander turns to me. "Perhaps we should go over some rules of engagement while we're in there."

I turn my head to face him. "Such as?"

Alexander presses the button on his door and effectively rolls up the privacy wall, separating us from the driver.

"Kissing for one," he says coolly. "It will be expected of us once we get in there. People are going to want to see some level of affection displayed toward one another."

"I'm pretty sure we'll be able to handle some simple pecks on the cheek. Seriously, Alexander, you're overthinking this. People will buy that we're together."

"How can you be so sure?" he asks. "Maybe we better practice a couple of kisses just to make sure we're on the same page. I don't feel like getting smacked in the middle of a party if I do something to offend you. I need to know what your limits are."

I level my stare on him. "You're really asking me to kiss you right now?"

He licks his lips and then beckons me with the crook of his finger. "Come here."

As ridiculous as this idea seems, he might just have a point based on our history. When we touch, crazy things happen. Setting boundaries between us is a good idea.

I sigh and then slide over toward him. Alexander's eyes trail down my body, taking a moment to stare at my chest. This low-cut Prada dress accentuates my breasts nicely, so I can't fault him for his lingering gaze.

He tilts his head and then places his hand on the bare skin of my thigh. "Will doing this get me smacked?"

My heart thunders inside my chest. The heat from the contact of his skin on mine is sending my body into overdrive.

"No," I tell him with a breathy tone. "But if you go any higher than that, it might."

"Noted." He arches one eyebrow. "How about this?" He moves his hand from my thigh and then cups my cheek. The pad of his thumb swirls around my skin before it dips lower to brush the corner of my mouth.

My mouth drifts open, and I close my eyes as he traces my lower lip with his thumb. An ache between my legs builds. It's crazy how my body reacts so quickly with one simple touch from this man.

I don't even realize he's leaning into me until I feel his warm breath on my face. "You don't know how badly I want to kiss you right now."

"What's stopping you?" I ask, needing more of his skin on mine in that moment.

He leans his forehead against mine. "Don't tease me like that, Margo."

"Who's teasing?" My hand snakes up his chest until it finds the exposed flesh on his neck. "I want you to kiss me."

He cups my face. "What are you doing to me? Why can't I resist you?"

I bite my lip as I gaze into his eyes. "I've asked myself the same thing about a million times. I'm supposed to hate you, but I can't stop wanting you."

That was easier to admit to him that I ever thought it would be.

Alexander sucks a rush of air in through his nose and his chest heaves. He doesn't move away from me, only stretches his hand out and hits the intercom button, simply instructing, "Drive."

"Where to, sir?" the driver asks.

"I don't give a fuck where. Drive until I tell you to stop," he orders.

The words no sooner leave his mouth than both of his hands are cradling my head, holding me in place while he crushes his lips to mine. His tongue swipes against my lips, begging for entrance while the trim whiskers on his face poke me. I moan as I open my mouth and welcome him inside.

This is wrong, but I can't find a reason within me to stop. It feels too good—too right.

His hand slides down my neck and then sweeps across my collarbone before pushing the straps of my dress off my shoulders. "I want you, Margo. Tell me that you want me, too."

His admission causes my blood to pump a little faster through my veins, and his need to hear my confirmation has every inch of me on fire. This man has a way of turning me on like no other, and he's damn near impossible to resist.

I grip the collar of his crisp white tuxedo shirt and stare into his eyes as I straddle his lap. The bottom hem of my dress rides up my thighs as I press myself against the hard erection in his pants. "I need you, Alexander."

Those simple words are all the permission that he needs. Alexander attacks my lips with his once again, while his hands work frantically to get me out of this dress. The need to have him inside me to stop my building ache is intense. I lift my bottom a bit to gain access to his belt. When that's out of the way, I make quick work of unzipping his pants and reaching inside his underwear. He lifts his hips, allowing me to shove the fabric down. I take his cock into my hand. The skin of his shaft is silky as I stroke his considerable length.

Alexander watches me carefully under his long lashes as he reaches between my legs and strokes my clit through the material of my underwear. "These panties are soaked. I love that you get that way for me. Tell me, Margo. When you pleasure yourself, do you think of me?"

My chest heaves as Alexander pushes my panties to the side and slides his finger against my most sensitive flesh. If he keeps this up, I might explode.

"Oh, God." I throw my head back and allow his naughty words to ring through my mind as I enjoy his touch.

"Do you think of this, Margo? Do you long for it? Do you touch yourself and wish it was me?"

I bite my bottom lip while I curl my fingers around his cock. I can't concentrate on anything but my own pleasure and the way he's making me feel. He has me so turned on I can't see straight.

"I've missed this." He leans in and licks the soft skin just below my ear. "When I don't have you, I'm dreaming of fucking you, tasting your lips, and hearing you scream my name while you come all over my tongue."

Fire pools in the pit of my belly. I lean in and kiss him before moaning into his mouth. "Alexander . . ."

"Tell me, Margo. Do you want me inside you?" he murmurs.

"Yesss," I hiss.

He moves his hand, leaving my underwear pushed to the side and then pulls me back on top of him. The warmth of his cock against my clit feels so damn good. I rock against him a few times, coating him with my desire and allowing our skin to slide together with ease.

Alexander goes to work, trying to undo the zipper in the back of my dress. He curses when it sticks halfway down and then tugs roughly on the dress, losing all patience with taking his time in getting me naked.

The distinct sound of the fabric ripping causes my head to snap up. "My dress!"

Panic shoots through me, knowing I won't be able to go into the gala like this.

Alexander threads his fingers through my hair and locks me into place. The tip of his nose traces my jawline, breathing me in as he continues his deliciously slow torture of teasing me.

"I'll buy you a fucking new one. Don't you dare stop," he growls in my ear.

I do exactly as he commands and continue rocking my hips. He shoves the torn fabric down, allowing it to pool around my hips. His patience with my underwear seems to be gone too because he reaches under my dress and rips them away from my body.

The index finger of his right hand dips into the cup of my bra. It twirls around my nipple before moving on to the next. He bites his lip as he pushes the cups of my strapless bra down, fully exposing my breasts. His tongue darts out and licks the taut pink flesh before he sucks the entire thing into his mouth.

Every nerve in my body comes to life, and I thread my fingers into his thick, dark hair. I rock against him, needing to feel him inside me. "I'm so ready."

Alexander grips my hips, steadying me against him. "I want to feel you, Margo. I want to come inside you this time."

My mind drifts back to the time when we had sex against the door in Vegas and how amazing that felt. That also reminds me this is the second dress he's ruined during sex. He's technically my husband and I'm on birth control, so I don't see the harm in it just this once.

I nod as I play with a strand of his hair that's poking out in the back. "Okay."

He leans in and presses his lips to mine as he shifts his hips and his cock presses against my entrance. A quick thrust of his hips and he slips his dick inside me all the way up to the base.

His mouth drifts open, and he stares up at me with lust-coated eyes as he works my hips in a slow rhythm. "Fuck. So damn amazing."

We rock in time, both getting lost in our own desire—both searching for our own release.

Watching him as he enjoys my body is one of the hottest things I've ever seen. I like knowing that I can cause the asshole control freak, Alexander King, to lose all control. It's powerful and liberating and makes me feel downright sexy.

It doesn't take long before that familiar tingle overtakes every inch of my being. "Oh, that's it," I pant. "Oh, God. Alexander, I'm coming."

No sooner do the words leave my lips do I fall apart, giving in to the wave of pleasure that Alexander's given me.

He tightens his grip on my hips and works them faster and faster until he's biting his lip and sweat beads on his forehead. We lock eyes and a low growl escapes his lips as he explodes inside me, filling me full with his desire.

We stay wrapped in one another's arms, staring into each other's eyes as we try to catch our breath. I don't know what just happened, but this sexual encounter with him felt different—more intimate—and it feels like everything is about to change.

Chapter XI
MAY I CUT IN?

Margo

AFTER A CHANGE OF CLOTHES at Alexander's apartment, I'm heading back down the stairs. Hopefully, we make it to the event this time. I glance at my phone before dropping it into my clutch. We're running extremely late.

When I meet Alexander in the foyer, he takes my hand. The warmth of his fingers curled around mine feels so intimate. I'm not sure what in the hell happened between us back in that limo, but it's more apparent to me now that keeping things strictly business between the two of us is impossible. Something just happens when we're together. There's a pull—a connection—I don't understand, and I'm pretty sure Alexander feels it, too. Otherwise, he wouldn't have allowed himself to end up married to me, causing himself a whole lot of grief in the process. He's too smart for that, which is how I know the brain behind that beautiful face of his isn't making the decisions when it comes to me.

I glance down at our hands as we make our way outside to the waiting limo. I'm tempted to ask him if he's merely pretending to show me public affection for the benefit of anyone who's watching or if he's holding my hand because he wants to, but I won't. I don't want to know the answer. If he claims it's just an act, it might hurt.

Inside the limo, I expect for Alexander to pull away from me, but he doesn't. We ride to the gala side by side, still holding hands like a happily married couple.

As we pull up to the building the party is being held in, Alexander turns his head toward me while wearing a devilish smirk. "You ready to try this again, or are you ready for round two?"

A blush creeps over my cheeks. As much as I would love nothing more than to go another round with him, I know there's simply no time for that. Tonight is all about convincing the board members of King Corporation that Alexander is more than capable of running the empire his father left behind.

"As much as I'd like that, we have a job to do," I tell him. "But I'll take a rain check on that second round."

Alexander's smile widens. "Are you sure? I wouldn't want to make your battery operated boyfriend jealous."

I chuckle at his reference to my vibrator. "Don't worry. B.O.B. only wants to see me satisfied. He's probably enjoying the vacation."

"Bob might have to go. You know I'm a jealous man. I don't share, especially when it comes to you." He reaches over and slides one hand between my legs and then brushes my panty-covered folds with his thumb. "And this pussy is all mine."

His words cause me to shiver. Never have I been claimed like this before, and I have to admit, it's a fucking turn-on.

"Tonight, I want you in my bed." Alexander leans in and brushes my lips with his. "But first, we have a little business to handle inside. Are you ready?"

"Let's do this."

A few lingering paparazzi snap photos of Alexander and me as we step out of the car—all of them clamoring for a shot of us to put in the society gossip columns.

"Mr. King, is it true that the two of you are married?" one heavyset, balding man with a camera shouts, but Alexander doesn't even bother to glance in his direction.

Sure, I've been in the society papers before, but no one has ever been desperate to know so much about my personal life. It's weird that people would even care, but things are different for Alexander. He's been on the public radar since he was named youngest billionaire in the world ten years ago when he inherited his father's company. People are fascinated by handsome young men who are extremely wealthy.

Alexander reminds tight-lipped until we make it inside the building. "I'm sure we're going to get a lot of that until the shock over our marriage dies down. As soon as they find another big story to cover, they'll forget about us." He extends his elbow to me, and I loop my arm through his. "Come on. Let's get this ass-kissing over with. The sooner we can get away from these pretentious assholes, the better."

I can't help but laugh. His blunt vocabulary is actually comical when I'm not pissed at him for talking to me that way.

The ballroom is alive with Manhattan's upper-crust society, milling about in their small cliques. A jazz band plays in the corner and a few couples are dancing while everyone else lingers about gossiping or discussing business ventures. A few heads turn in our direction, and it doesn't go unnoticed that I'm clinging to Alexander's arm.

The men in the room nod as if approving Alexander's choice of arm candy for the night, but the women are a completely different story. Their expressions range from pity to contempt. I'm guessing the ones who look like they want to punch me in the face are women Alexander has slept with and aren't quite over him yet.

"I feel like everyone's staring at us," I whisper.

Alexander rubs the light beard covering his face. "Angry beehive, remember? This is where we'll need to sell it most." He gazes down at me. "I'm going to kiss you now. It's best to get this over with. Let them know where we stand, just as we did at the office the other day."

He's right. It will save me from having to explain our relationship status a million different times for the next hour.

I nod. "Okay."

Alexander pinches my chin gently between his thumb and forefinger. "The countdown clock to get you into my bed starts now."

A genuine smile spreads across my face. "Looking forward to it."

He leans down and presses his lips to mine, and the weight of all the eyes in the room judging us falls on my shoulders. The kiss doesn't last long, and it isn't more than a sweet peck, but it's enough to show everyone in this room there is definitely something going on between us.

Alexander pulls back. "Let's work this room."

And that's exactly what we do. We spend the next hour rubbing elbows with some of the wealthiest people in New York. Most of the board members appear to be pleased with the match between Alexander and me. All but one, that is.

A tall, slender blond woman with a little age on her approaches us with a smile, but I can tell right away that it's not genuine. It's a forced act for Alexander's benefit as she leans in and kisses him on both cheeks. "Alexander, darling, how nice to see you."

Alexander's posture is notably different. His stance has gone from relaxed to rigid.

Something about this woman obviously puts his guard up.

The woman's eyes instantly flit over to me after she releases Alexander. "Are you going to introduce me to your date?"

His nostrils flare as he inhales deeply. "Camille, this is Margo Buchanan—my wife."

Camille's dark green eyes widen. "Your wife? Wow." She turns her attention to me and extends her hand. "You'll have to excuse my surprise. When Alexander dated my daughter, Jess, he never really seemed like the type to ever settle down. It's hard for me to picture Alexander as a married man."

I swallow down the lump in my throat. I never anticipated on meeting anyone connected to Alexander's ex tonight. Especially not the one I've been told who broke his heart. It's difficult to digest that the man I'm starting to open myself up to and feel something for was once very much in love with someone else. I'm jealous this woman exists and probably had a relationship with the easygoing Alexander I've witnessed from time to time. It's also hard for me to grasp the reason Alexander is the way he is with women is because of Jess according to Yamada.

I want to get back at this girl for hurting Alexander, even though I don't know her at all.

I turn and lean into Alexander, placing my right hand on his chest as I address Camille. "I keep hearing that my Alexander was quite the ladies' man, but I assure you he's a changed man." I flick my gaze back up to Alexander's smile. "He has my heart completely and I have his. We're each other's everything."

"How lovely, for you." There's a hardened edge to her voice. "I hope that it stays that way."

I level my gaze on Camille and the smile drops off my face while I place my left hanf on Alexander's chest to show off the ring he just gave me. "Thank you for your concern, but I assure you it's unnecessary. We're completely in love with one another and will be very happy together. Nothing will get in the way of that."

Her lips twist and I can tell that she despises me and wants nothing more than to tell me off. I don't understand why she would hold ill will toward Alexander. Her daughter is the one who dumped him. She can't possibly be upset that he's moved on with his life.

Instead of saying another word to me, Camille turns on her heel and storms away from us. The sparkly dress she's wearing trail behind her.

I turn back to Alexander. "That was odd. What's her deal?"

Alexander wraps his arm around my waist, drawing me in tightly against his side. "She wanted her daughter to marry me. She didn't exactly approve of the tennis pro that she ran off with when she left me. He doesn't make enough money to suit Camille's standards."

"So why blame you? Clearly the split with her daughter isn't your fault."

"She knows that, but it doesn't stop her from blaming me. Jess can do no wrong according to her parents, so no matter the situation, it's always going to be someone else's fault—never Jess's."

"That's crazy," I say.

"Agreed, but that's how things work around here. You know that. Family is always going to defend their blood no matter what." He kisses the top of my head. "Let's get out of here. Kissing ass here tonight chapped my lips, and I've had enough of these people for one night. Besides, I do believe we're on a tight schedule for the rest of our plans for the evening."

One side of my mouth pulls up into a grin as I think about all the naughty things he's going to do to my body when we get back to his place. Being married to Alexander King does come with some perks.

Chapter XII
YAMADA'S BOOTY PARADISE

Alexander

I KNEW MARGO WAS STRONG, but I never realized how protective she was until she stood up to Jess's mother two nights ago. It felt nice to hear her brag about how much she was into me, even if she didn't mean it.

Time flew by after that night. It's been much easier than I anticipated to be happily married to Margo Buchanan. In fact, it's gotten so easy that the lines of what's real between us have been blurred. The first word that comes to mind when I think of Margo is no longer hate. I've become quite fond of her, and when the time comes for us to part ways, I'll actually miss her. It's not just the sex I'll miss either. I'll miss how that smart mouth of hers is always there to call me out for being an asshole, and I'll miss her audacity.

I flip her over onto her stomach, yank her to the edge of the bed, and smack her ass with the palm of my hand. She groans just like she did when I spanked her last time. She's a dirty girl underneath that tough persona.

She's the perfect example of the old saying about being a lady in the streets and a freak in the sheets.

I slam my cock back into her tight pussy, causing her to moan. I grip her shoulders and continue to pound into her, searching desperately for my release.

I have to admit that having a bedroom on my private jet comes in quite handy during long flights like this and keeps me from putting on a show for the crew.

She curls her fingers around the sheets as her entire body shakes. "Oh, God. I'm coming. I'm coming. Alexander . . ."

Hearing my name roll off her lips while she's in the midst of ecstasy never gets old. I love making her come. It's highly addictive to witness and even more intoxicating to know that I'm the one making her feel so damn good.

It's not long before every nerve inside me starts tingling, and I explode inside her, filling her full.

I lean down, pressing my chest against her back while I catch my breath. I bite the bare skin on her shoulder and then kiss the exact spot. "I swear it gets better every single time we fuck."

Margo shakes her head, causing her long dark curls to bounce around. "I wish you wouldn't refer to what we are doing as fucking. It sounds so . . ."

"So what?" I probe.

"Graphic."

I pull out of her and then lie down next to her. "What would you have me call it then? Making love?"

She props her head up with her hand and stares down at me. "Don't be ridiculous. We're not in love."

"Exactly," I say. "Which is why it makes perfect sense to refer to it as fucking. We get each other off. It's what we do. We fuck."

She's quiet for a few moments, but then nods. "I suppose you're right."

I pull her to me and kiss her forehead as she lays her head on my chest, effectively ending that topic of conversation.

I trace the bare skin on her shoulder and try to memorize the softness of it because I know sharing moments like this with Margo is a fleeting pastime.

We both lie there in silence—neither of us saying what it is that's running through our mind—both of us knowing that this thing between us is only temporary.

My cell phone on the nightstand rings, and I debate on whether I should answer the call or stay wrapped up just like this.

"Are you going to get that?" Margo asks as she tilts her head up so she can look at me.

I smile down at her as I pull away and reach for the cell on the nightstand. "King."

"Where are you, asshole? It's almost midnight. When Yamada says be here Thursday, it doesn't mean show up Friday morning."

I sigh. "I know. We got a late start. I had a few things to wrap up at the office before we headed out tonight. We'll be there soon enough."

"Okay, but I don't want this weekend to turn out like Vegas where you spend the entire time playing eat the cookie with Dime Piece." There's irritation in his voice. "Yamada expects a huge party this time."

"You got it. And I promise tomorrow we'll party, but just give me tonight alone with Margo when we get there."

I know that I flew out here to spend the weekend with him and secure the Buchanan deal for his company, but I don't want to pull myself away from Margo tonight.

"Okay. Yamada will give you your fuck night with Dime Piece, but tomorrow you assholes better be ready because Yamada has a big surprise for you."

I chuckle. "Don't worry, buddy. We'll get it out of our systems tonight. Tomorrow, you'll have our undivided attention."

"Oh, sexy, sexy. Can Yamada video you? We put that shit on the Internet and make you famous. Dime Piece could be a centerfold model."

"Good night, Yamada." I quickly cut him off before he expands his idea about showing Margo's body off to the world because I fucking hate the very idea of that.

"Is he upset?" Margo asks.

I stare down at her and run my fingers through her thick hair. "No, just seemed disappointed. I wouldn't worry too much about him, though. Yamada is pretty resilient. The man loves a good party, and it doesn't matter who it's with most of the time."

"He said you two went to college together." It's a statement, not a question.

"It's hard to picture the two of you as such good friends."

I smile as I think back on the night I met Yamada. "It's hard not to like the little asshole. He has a way of making you have so much fun that you don't care how absolutely ridiculous you look while doing it. The first night I met him, he was able to talk me into doing a few keg stands in order to get noticed by a girl."

"Was it Jess?" she asks, and instantly, my body stiffens.

"How do you know about her?"

It wasn't a secret. Those who know me well knew I was in a long-term relationship with Jess, but I don't like to talk about it. Some things need to stay fucking buried because they hurt too damn much.

"Yamada . . ." She shrugs.

Figures. He never did know how to keep his mouth shut. Now, I need to figure out exactly what my friend has been telling her about me.

"What did he say?"

"Not much," she admits. "He only said that I was the second girl who you were ever able to get before him—Jess was the first, but then she broke your heart."

I blow a rush of air out of my nose. "I don't like to talk about her."

Margo chews the inside corner of her lower lip. "I can respect that. Relationships suck. Promises aren't always kept and people get hurt, which is why I decided a long time ago that I never wanted to fall in love."

"That's good that you protect yourself because love is for suckers." I trace the contours of her beautiful face and wish that I didn't believe that. "I'm glad we both can see what we're doing here for the physicality of it and nothing more."

There's a flicker of pain in her expression before she nods. "It's good we've both agreed this is just fucking then."

My heart squeezes at that thought. Suddenly, I wish I had never said that. I didn't mean to make her think that what was happening between us didn't mean anything to me because it does. While I'm certainly not in love, I do feel a definite attachment to her. It would be so easy to fall for Margo if I allowed myself to open up, but deep down, we both know a relationship between us would never work. We're both too controlling, and when I go behind her back and make this deal with

Yamada to tear her father's company apart, she'll hate me even more than she ever did. I know it. That's why this has to be just fucking. That's why, as much as I want to have her in my bed just like this every damn night, it can never happen. However, I have the urge to at least let her know this time we have spent together meant something to me.

"Would it be strange to say I'm no longer excited by the thought of divorcing you?"

She shakes her head. "I was just thinking the same thing. It's weird to say that I would like to date my husband."

I chuckle. "It definitely does sound odd when you put it like that. As much as I would like to say we could try dating, I think we should wait and see how things go between us for a while. I mean, it was only last week that you hated my guts."

"That's true. Perhaps you're right."

A cocky grin spreads over my face. "I usually am."

She rolls her eyes and then pushes herself up from the bed and heads to the bathroom.

A few hours later, we're in a helicopter heading toward Yamada's island. He's going to be pissed that we're here so late, but I know he'll eventually get over it.

I've never seen a sunrise like this before. The sky lights up as the sun pops up above the rippling water, lighting up the ocean as far as the eye can see. The turquoise waters meet the multicolored sky. I'll give the little shit one thing. He picked one of the most beautiful places on the planet to buy an island.

"It's beautiful," Margo exclaimed into the microphone that's attached to the headset. "It's been so long since I've been to the beach. I'm actually looking forward to this."

"Let me guess. You were too busy earning two degrees that you didn't get out."

She nods. "Yep. That's exactly right."

I smile at her. "In that case, Princess, I'm going to make it my personal mission to see that you have a good time while you're out here."

Finally, a small island comes into view. Trees cover the tall, rolling hills of most of the place, but there are some visible paths and roads, not to mention the large resort sitting along the back shoreline.

This is the kind of place where famous people come to party out of the spotlight.

The chopper hovers over the landing pad and then steadily descends. Yamada sits in a white topless Jeep that has no doors while he waits for us to land.

When we're on the ground, the crew opens the door and helps us out. We duck as we walk over to Yamada.

"Get in, madafakas. Yamada's been waiting for you all night."

I glance over at Margo, and she shrugs before climbing into the backseat. Looks like she's learned quickly to just go with whatever Yamada has in mind.

I follow suit and climb into the passenger seat. My ass no sooner hits the seat before Yamada mashes the gas, sending us shrieking down the dirt road.

"Whoa!" I grab the dashboard and reach for the seat belt to buckle myself in. The last thing I need is to fall out of a speeding vehicle because of Yamada's crazy driving. "Have you slept at all since I spoke to you last night?"

"Sleep?" he says with a chuckle. "No time for that. Yamada was busy entertaining. Everyone Yamada knows is here to celebrate my new island. Those madafakas are still up partying."

I furrow my brow. "Who did you invite?"

"Everyone," he emphasizes. "I put the invite out to all my friends on social media, and most of them showed up."

"Jesus. Social media? You'll have every freak you've ever met here." I pinch the bridge of my nose. I don't know why I expected this to be a quiet weekend because I know how Yamada is. He's not the type who only attends a party—he is the party.

He reaches over and grabs my shoulder, giving it a little shake. "Don't worry, King. You special. Yamada saved you and Dime Piece a room. The rest of the assholes here have to sleep in tents."

I shake my head at my crazy friend.

The massive main house that we spotted from the helicopter comes into view, and my jaw drops as I take in the crowd gathered around front. Yamada wasn't kidding when he said he invited everyone. There are bodies wearing only bikinis and swimming trunks as far as the eye can see.

Yamada whips the Jeep into a parking spot right in front of the house and then pops up out of his seat. "Yamada's back, bitches. Get the music started. Time to celebrate this wedding right!"

The crowd cheers and most of the people hold up cups of beer.

My eyes widen. "What is this, Yamada?"

Yamada jumps out of the Jeep then turns to me and grins. "Best man's job is to throw parties, and who better to throw you a reception than Yamada?"

I step out of the vehicle and help Margo out. I open my mouth to tell Yamada that we didn't need a party—that our marriage was a mistake and now it's part of a business deal, nothing more—but Margo places her hand on my chest, stopping me from saying anything at all.

"That's very nice of you, Yamada. Thank you," Margo tells him and then pats me on the chest. "We appreciate it."

This seems to please him because his smile grows wider. "Welcome. Now, let's party."

He takes us both by the hand and leads us into the awaiting crowd. Most of the people among all these dancing bodies are people I've never seen before, but leave it to Yamada to throw a rager on a private island.

Some hip-hop song blasts through the speakers, and while Yamada busies himself rapping along to the song, I grind against Margo.

She smiles as she wraps her arms around my neck and swings her hips to the beat. It's the first time since Vegas that we've had fun like this, and it's nice.

After a few more songs, Margo pushes up on her tiptoes to talk into my ear. "I'm going to get a drink. Do you want anything?"

"A beer would be great. Thank you." It's a nice gesture for her to think of me.

I smile as I watch her walk off toward the bar inside the house. Who knew Margo Buchanan would end up being so nice to me. I follow behind her, not wanting her to feel like she has to fetch me a drink like she does at work. I cringe at the thought that delegating that task made her feel like a servant. It was wrong of me, and I won't ask her to do it again.

When I approach the bar, the first thing I see is a man standing next to Margo a little too close for my liking. He turns toward her and leans his side against the bar so that he can fix his gaze on her. I can tell by the way he's watching her that he's thinking about making a move, but what he doesn't know is that she's already been taken. By me.

The guy is about my height, with about twenty pounds or so on me, but that doesn't matter. If he makes a move on Margo, he'll lose a fucking arm.

The bartender takes Margo's order and then turns his attention to the guy next to Margo and asks him for his order. "Bud Light, and buy this pretty woman next to me another round of whatever she just ordered."

"No thanks," Margo says stiffly.

The guy touches her arm, and I just lose my fucking head. There's no way in hell I am going to stand here and allow another man to touch what's mine.

I shove his hand away and step between Margo and him. "She said no, motherfucker. Hit the fucking road."

The man's face turns white as a sheet, and he takes a step back. "Sorry, man. Didn't know she was claimed."

"Beat it, pussy," is all I say to cause the man to turn tail and run.

"Aww, shit. Yamada missed another King throw down. Damn, it's sexy when you get all fired up," Yamada teases. "Next time an ass kicking is brewing, come get Yamada. We can throw down."

I laugh. "Next time, they're all yours."

That seems to satisfy him because he turns and disappears into the crowd, leaving Margo and me standing there.

I pull her into my arms. "You all right?"

"Never better." She turns her gaze up to look me in the eyes and smiles. "He cares about you a lot. It's really clicking why the two of you are such good friends because I'll admit, I didn't understand your relationship at first. The two of you are very different."

"I don't know how our friendship works, but it just does."

"Sometimes people have a way of worming themselves into your heart whether you want them to or not."

I continue to gaze into her eyes, and I can't help but feel a little hopeful that she means me even though I shouldn't. It's wrong of me to want her to feel something for me because I know that I'm about to break her heart. But I'm a selfish bastard and I'll hope for it anyway.

I lean in and press my lips to hers. "I'm glad we're here together."

"Me, too," an all too familiar voice purrs from behind me.

I whip around just in time to see a blast from my past standing there in nothing but a black string bikini.

"What are you doing here?" Even I can hear the shock in my voice as I drop my hands from around Margo's waist and pull away from her.

"I had to come and see for myself if the Naughty King is married." Jess tilts her head, swinging her long, blond ponytail. She looks just the same as the last time I saw her—drop-dead gorgeous. But that wicked smile of hers doesn't fool me. This woman broke my heart—she taught me that no woman could be trusted.

Her presence reminds me that I've been allowing Margo inside my heart too much. I have to get back to being an asshole. I've already lowered my guard too much around her, and it's caused me a lot of fucking trouble.

My back stiffens. "So you've seen it. Now, fucking leave."

Jess smirks. "Oh, I'm not going anywhere. Not until I'm convinced the two of you are in love and it's not some fucking charade. Daddy says that he and the rest of the board could take full control if they can prove you were out making careless decisions with your personal life."

"Fuck your father," I snarl. "I'll fuck Margo right here in front of you to prove that we're married for real."

Jess shakes her head. "Fucking her won't prove anything. I need to be convinced you love her. Who better to judge if Alexander King is in love than the last woman he asked to marry him?"

Margo gasps next to me and then turns to storm off. I snatch her wrist, halting her in place. "Now is not the time for a temper tantrum."

She jerks out of my grasp. "Don't tell me what to do, King."

"Margo. Come back here."

She doesn't look back as she storms away.

I scrub my hand down my face. I don't know what in the hell she's mad about, but I decide not to chase her down and cause a scene, especially not in front of Jess.

"Looks like trouble in paradise," Jess says in a singsong voice beside me.

My nostrils flare as I turn my heated gaze on her. "Shut the fuck up, Jess. I don't know why you feel the need to interfere with my life. You left me, remember? Leave me the hell alone."

Jess steps up to me and grins. "I can't leave you alone. This time, it's not personal, baby. It's business. My daddy needs me to expose your little lie, and I need to prove to everyone that it's me who you still really love, not that uptight feisty princess."

"Stay. Away. From. Me," I say my words slowly with enough intensity so she knows how fucking serious I am.

She lifts one eyebrow and then walks away.

When she's out of sight, I set out to find Yamada. It doesn't take long to find him by the pool with a girl on his lap and one on each side of him.

I storm over to him, seething. "What in the fuck is Jess doing here?"

"Calm down, King. I told you everyone was here. Besides, Jess knows you with Dime Piece now. She's just here to party with Yamada like old times and help break in Yamada's new island."

I rake my fingers through my hair. I love Yamada, but sometimes he can be so blind to the ulterior motives people have. He's too quick to believe the good in people even when they don't deserve it.

"That's not why she's here. She's here to spy on me for her father who sits on the fucking board of my company. She's trying to prove that my marriage is a sham so the board can overthrow my power."

"Then just show her that you in love with Dime Piece. Everything fixed."

"It's not that simple, and you know it."

Yamada pushes the girl off his lap, and he stands. "Course it is, King. You are in love. Yamada knows it and so do you. You just won't admit it to yourself."

I flinch. "I don't—"

"Okay then, Yamada is going to go in there and try to get into Dime Piece's panties."

I throw my hands up, palms out. "Whoa. Let's not get crazy."

"See!" he exclaims. "You only get jealous when you care. You. Are. In. Love."

My lips pull into a tight line. No. That can't be right. Can it? Me? In love? That's preposterous. I don't do love, or at least I thought I didn't. But I do know that I care about Margo. A lot. I care about hurting her, which is why I'm wrestling with the plan I have to betray her when it comes to the deal I made with her.

Yamada gives my shoulder a firm pat. "Go talk to Margo. Tell her you love her. It make things better. You see."

He's right. I do need to speak with her, but I'm not ready to admit that I feel something for her. I'm not even sure about my own feelings at this point.

"I'm going to go," I tell him.

I turn on my heel and set out to find Margo. The crowd is thick, but I know she won't be in the middle of it, so I begin checking every secluded place I can find. When I round the outside corner of the building, my eyes land on one of my very best friends and my baby sister. They are sitting too close for my fucking comfort on a bench built for two. Jack and Diem sit side-by-side with their heads lowered, talking privately. My sister glances over at Jack and smiles. I don't like that smile. It's too flirty, and I'll be damned if I allow anything to happen between the two of them.

"What the hell is this?" I ask, not moving my eyes off them.

Diem jumps up instantly from her seat. "Hey! Alexander! Some party, right?"

I narrow my eyes. "Don't change the fucking subject, Diem. Why are the two of you doing that?"

"We weren't doing anything, Alexander. You are too damn paranoid. Nothing is going on."

My eyes flick to Jack for a second before they return back to my sister. I don't have time for this bullshit. I have to find Margo. "Squash this shit. Now. It's not happening between the two of you. Ever."

I curl my fingers into fists, and I feel the need to lash out. Everything feels like it's coming down on me at once, and I feel like I'm about to lose my goddamn mind.

Jack pushes himself up off the bench and approaches me slowly with his hands up in surrender. "What's wrong, man? You look panicked."

I rub the skin on the back of my neck, willing myself to calm down and refocus on the major issue at hand. "Jess is here to spy on me for her fucking father, trying to prove that my marriage is a complete fucking fake."

"I spoke with the board, Alexander. I don't think you have anything to worry about. Everyone seemed really pleased with your marriage to Margo after the King

Gala, which tells me they all are buying your story. We just need to ride this out for a few more days, and then we're in the home stretch. So do the best you can to stay away from Jess until then."

"Okay. I have to find Margo and make sure she's still on the same page. I just pissed her off. I have to make sure she's okay."

Jack nods. "She actually just passed by here. She was on her phone. You better go find her in case she was arranging a flight back to New York."

"Shit. All right. I'll see you two in a bit," I tell them before I rush off in search of Margo.

Panic sets in. I can't allow her to leave here mad at me. I need to find her and apologize.

That last thought stops me dead in my tracks. When in the fuck did I start having the urge to tell someone I was sorry? I'm Alexander King. I'm not supposed to be sorry for anything I do, but this time I am. I don't like the idea of hurting Margo in any way.

It's not until I walk down to the beach that I find her. She's staring out at the sea while the waves crash around her ankles.

I step up beside her and notice the tears streaming down her face. While I know it was shitty to keep something like that from her, I never took Margo for one who would cry over it.

It makes me feel bad that I hurt her like that.

I swallow hard. "I knew I should've told you that I proposed to Jess—"

"I don't give a shit about what you did in your past. I walked away because I'm tired of you thinking you can just use my body any time you feel like it. Don't you ever use fucking me as leverage again."

"Margo, that was just a threat to prove to her how serious I am about you."

"Whatever. Just don't do it again."

That's a reasonable request. "Okay. I won't."

I figured that would make the tears stop, but they continue to flow down her face. It worries me, so I put my arm around her shoulders. "I said I wouldn't do it again. You can stop crying now."

She shakes her head and her lips pull into a tight line. "That's not it."

I give her shoulders a little squeeze. "What is it then? Tell me. Maybe I can make whatever it is better."

"Not this," she whispers. "My dad's dead."

My eyes widen. "What? How?"

"Heart attack," she says simply. "My father's attorney just called me. Apparently, I have to sign some paperwork making me the new head of Buchanan Industries immediately."

I wrap her in my arms and comfort her the best way I know how. "I'm so sorry, Margo. I know he meant a great deal to you. We'll leave as soon as you need to."

She sobs into my chest as I stroke her hair, attempting to soothe her pain. It kills me to see her cry like this because I've lost a parent, too. It hurts like a motherfucker.

I wish I can do more, but no matter how much money I have, it won't bring her dad back. I wish it would though because I would've brought mine back a long time ago.

It's hard for me to even wrap my head around the fact that her father is dead.

My mind races through all the things that Dan Buchanan dying means to the deal I was about to strike with him for his company. My heart does a double thump in my ribs when one piece of the Buchanan puzzle pops into place. Since we're legally married, I now have rights to Buchanan Industries just as she has rights to King Corporation.

This fucking changes everything.

END PART TWO

Dirty Royals (A Sexy Manhattan Fairytale Part III)

Coming Soon

About the Author

NEW YORK TIMES AND USA Today Best Selling author Michelle A. Valentine is a Central Ohio nurse turned author of erotic and New Adult romance novels. Her love of hard-rock music, tattoos and sexy musicians inspires her naughty novels.

Find her:
Website: **www.michelleavalentine.com**
Facebook:
www.facebook.com/AuthorMichelleAValentine
Twitter: @M_A_Valentine